ELECTRIC SEWER

ELECTRIC SEWER

Edited by Thurston Howl
Book design by Thurston Howl

First edition, 2020.

A Thurston Howl Publications Book
Published by Thurston Howl Publications
thurstonhowlpublications.com
Fernandina Beach, FL

ELECTRIC SEWER

EDITED BY THURSTON HOWL

A THURSTON HOWL PUBLICATIONS BOOK

CONTENTS

NOT ENOUGH

THIGER

SHARP

THURSTON HOWL

POISONS

MIXED TAPE

VIP LOUNGE

WELCOME AND RULES

Hello, and welcome to the Electric Sewer!

Our fine establishment has served the fuzzy underbelly of our lovely town for the past ten years, and we hope to continue to service you.

For those who are new to the club, please note the rules, just so you know what you are getting into:

This is a clothing-optional space. No kids. No cops. Things get sexy in here.

This is an alcohol-friendly space. Don't bother coming in if you're not legal age.

This is a drug-friendly space. Fuck the police.

Shit happens here. <u>If you got major problems seeing blood, sex, violence, sexual assault, dubious consent, lack of consent, sexual mutilation, and gore, then this might not be the place for you.</u>

Don't forget to tip your bartender.

And of course, have fun. Welcome to the night of your life. A night of Neon. Beats. Howling. Blood. Pumping. Intoxication. Riding that Mother-Fucking High. And Getting Bred Full of Pups.

Welcome to the Electric Sewer.

ELECTRIC GROOVE

THOMAS "FAUX" STEELE

The water streaming down my body runs red as blood. I glance at my reflection in the steam-clouded mirror. A handsome red fox greets me like a butterfly emerging from his chrysalis, having replaced the mild-mannered arctic fox that stepped in twenty minutes ago. I do a little twirl, admiring how the color running down my flanks accentuates the curves of my hips. It's the perfect costume for a night away from work.

I flip the shower off, letting the last warm rivulets trickle down my back. As I step out, a sharp jolt of pain needles me from a crick in the neck. I've been spending too many hours hunched over a computer desk. I gingerly rub my shoulder while peeling off the protective coating that kept portions of my white coat intact. As I scrutinize my dye job, I notice a few patches on where the dye has flown unevenly, leaving my fur more salmon then red. Something to improve upon next time I suppose.

I throw on a patterned button down and acid wash jeans, carefully combing my close-cropped headfur into a sleek, androgynous style. The Electric Sewer is a wild place, and deviating a little from the yuppie style of a county prosecutor might give me a little protection from the shady characters that hang around inside. I'm there to have a little fun, not get roughed up.

It's pitch black when I step outside, ready to head to where the action is. I blink a few times and then fold my Wayfarers into the breast pocket of my shirt. I guess I won't be wearing my sunglasses at night, not when the normally bright desert moon is blocked by bands of ominous clouds. My porch light has burned out again, making a dark night even darker. It's a brisk October evening, and the chill creeps through my Members Only jacket. My winter coat hasn't grown in yet, making me second-guess my decision not to go with something heavier. A chill creeps down my spine as unraked leaves rustle around the yard, colliding with barrel cacti and aloe vera plants.

After miraculously managing not to break my neck blindly descending the creaky wooden steps, I shimmy over to the midnight black Japanese wedge parked squarely in the driveway. Gleaming chrome TURBO badges on the fenders are the one bright spot on the bodywork. Behind me I hear a rustle, louder than before. My paw resting on the door handle, I quickly flip around, scanning the yard like a vigilant predator. It looks the same as always, the dilapidated shed I keep meaning to have replaced leering at me from the rear with shattered eyes.

It's probably just a feral jackrabbit. I nervously fumble the keys. They fall on the concrete with the discordant *ding* of a badly tuned windchime. I can't shake the feeling there's something intently gazing right at the nape of my neck. I scan the street as I slide the key into the lock, but there's no sign of life other than a lonely tumbleweed rolling through deserted suburbia. In the distance, a neglected billboard advertises some pop singer's end-of-career album. The neon strings of a gargantuan guitar pulse in time to the upbeat tempo of the lead single, but it looks wrong. One of the strings has burned out, jumbling the pattern up.

Once I manage to pop the lock, I rest my paw on the A-pillar and resolve not to let this weirdness ruin a good night out. I take a deep breath, gripping the steering wheel tight. I exhale and let the sensation pass as I slide the key into the ignition and bring the rotary engine to life. Pop-up headlights spring out from the hood, the dash lighting up in eye-piercing orange. I glance behind me, but the backseat contains only opposing counsel motions and empty Styrofoam coffee cups. I think I've been burning myself out. Perhaps I'm just suffering a dash of overwork-fueled paranoia.

I pop the clutch and shift into reverse, slowly rolling down my driveway. The firm suspension rattles my teeth as I bounce over the roots of the old mesquite tree by the mailbox. My paw nervously drums on the shift knob. There's a shrill howl in the distance, and then suddenly, silence. I fiddle with my radio until I hit on a station playing something synthetic, and then crank it up loud enough to drown out any ambient noise. I bob my head in time with the beat. Now this is just what I needed.

As I get onto the street and shift into first, I notice a set of quad headlamps flip on in my rearview mirror. They're just down the block, partially tucked behind a plumbing van. The deep blue sedan pulls out a few moments after I start rolling. I take a right at the stop sign at the end of my cul-de-sac. They stay close behind me. I'm blinded by intense white light as they tailgate me through another right turn onto the subdivision's main thoroughfare. I tap my fingers on the steering wheel as my mind flips through the possibilities. I've put away a lot of nasty men in my career. There's no shortage of gang members and mobsters who'd pay some crackhead to bash my brains in.

Just to make sure they're really tailing me, I drop my speed to below the limit. The car swerves around me. I peer over, and suddenly realize it's just my nearly blind ninety-year-old neighbor in her old land yacht. I breathe a sigh of relief and sink down into the cloth bucket seat, my tail wagging in relief against a thick volume of the Arizona Reports carelessly tossed back there. It was just my mind's paranoid machinations after all.

There's a sudden and violent shriek of metal-on-metal. My Mazda lurches forward, the engine whirring like an angry vacuum. My seatbelt barely prevents me from being impaled by the steering wheel. I gasp for air, my ribs throbbing. Behind me, American muscle snarls menacingly, dropping back to ram me again. Instinctively I slam the shifter into second and put my foot down, the rush of adrenaline clearing my mind.

My gut wasn't wrong after all.

The tachometer needle rushes towards redline as I pick up speed, wind noise pouring into the cabin. The turbo hisses with each shift, blowing off excess boost. I may not have the displacement, but I have the technology to give my pursuer a run for his money. I dart through traffic like a mouse through a kitchen. The cat keeps close behind, preventing me from putting more than a few car lengths between us.

I weigh my options and decide I-10 is my best chance of getting him off my tail. Jamming the parking brake, I slide onto the entrance ramp, mashing my foot to the floor as soon as I sense I have traction. I unleash the full forced-induction fury of the mighty little motor, and for a moment a grin creeps across my face. It evaporates as soon as the muscle car slams into me again. I jerk the wheel hard and let off the gas, barely avoiding fishtailing into the culvert off the shoulder. My tires shriek in protest as they spit gravel into the empty desert.

I manage to recover, but the black muscle car stays on me like a heat-seeking missile. I feel a knot of panic clenching my stomach. Up ahead, illuminated advertisements framing the asphalt strip beckon to drivers in vibrant neon. I focus on gaining speed as a figure on one of the new cathode ray tube billboards points to me and then holds up his Walkman. Leaving the speed limit far behind, I cut into the left lane and shift into fourth, my heart beating like the rapid-fire synth blasting through my stereo.

A harsh electronic chime breaks my concentration. I grab my carphone's handset from its mount on the dash as I weave around a tractor-trailer illegally hogging the passing lane. A phone call is exactly what I do not need right now.

"This is John Eubanks, Maricopa County Prosecutor's Office. Talk to me." The wind noise is so deafening I'm practically screaming into the mouthpiece.

The speedometer creeps into the triple digits. The black coupe is pacing me two lanes over, waiting for an opportunity to strike. "John, are you home right now?" It's one of my deputies, a down-to-business ferret named Melissa. Her voice is uncharacteristically mousy.

"No Mel, I'm out and about. Is this about De Luca? Please tell me you've managed to get him to take the plea bargain." We'd been working this case for months, trying to get him to flip with the mountain of evidence the undercover investigation had on him. We were damn close. De Luca was the mob's money man until we nabbed him, so his testimony would be worth its weight in gold. If she had managed to flip him, I could file enough RICO charges to take down the entire Romano crime family.

"No, it's about Simmons. John...he's dead." Her voice trembles a little. "There's a SWAT team en route to your house right now."

"What?" Momentarily frozen by a wave of raw, animalistic terror, I watch helplessly as the muscle car slams into the rear of a minivan in the center lane up ahead. It sloshes side-to-side for a moment as the driver fights for control. Just when I think it'll be okay, the driver overcorrects and loses it. The van's rear strikes the front of a tractor trailer and it rolls. I steer out of the way, but it's not fast enough. An infant's car seat smashes against the trailing edge of my passenger-side windshield, leaving a spiderweb of cracks and a smear of blood as it slides back onto the roadway. A moment later, it disappears under the back tires of an F-250 dually.

"John, are you still there? I said Simmons is dead." Merciless flames slowly shrink in my rearview mirror. I dodge around another grandma by swerving onto the shoulder. The rumble strips rattle my teeth and jingle the coins in the center console.

"What the fuck do you mean he's dead? Don't tell me it was a heart attack." Simmons liked to smoke a pack a day and was usually down a fifth of Scotch by lunchtime, but the coyote was magic at finding just the right case to back up our arguments.

"John, his wife just found him in about twelve different places around his house. I've never seen a killing so brutal. His guts were draped down the bannister like Christmas tinsel. They found his head in the bed. The killer fucked his eye socket John. His god-damned eye socket."

"Sweet Jesus Fox." I see my exit up ahead and decide to get off the freeway. Staying on the open road is suicide. "Did our guys apprehend a suspect?"

"Whoever did this was long gone by the time she found Simmons." The plastic earpiece is pressed so hard against my ear a little drop of blood spatters onto the center console lid. I can barely hear her over the wind and road noise, but I hang on every word. "Get yourself to a police station, now."

"That might be a bit of a problem, Mel." My right mirror detonates like a grenade. Another gunshot goes wild, shooting a shower of sparks onto the roadway from a billboard to my left. "Meet me at the Electric Sewer. Bring some firepower. You can get here faster than the police can. Go, now. I think the killer is after me."

I click the phone back into the cradle and grip the steering wheel so tightly my fingers start to go numb. I'm dodging through traffic with just inches to spare, flinching as I anticipate the violent scream of metal-on-metal every time I switch lanes. Another gunshot. My rear window bursts into shards. Wind whistles through the exposed louvers. I'm heading for the red-light district of Phoenix and there isn't a cop for miles around. I'm not sure they'd come if we offered them all the pink-frosted donuts the asset forfeiture slush fund could buy.

I'm on my own.

Before my pursuer can riddle my car with more bullets, I cut off a suit who is in a BMW and barely avoid plowing into the impact attenuator as I jam hard on the brakes to make my exit. I slow enough on the off ramp to make the corner without spinning out. Up ahead, the Electric Sewer beckons in faded neon glory. I'm heading into a rough neighborhood, there's no doubt about that. While the buildings are painted in bright purples and pinks, the homeless strewn along the sidewalk are as drab as a Charles Dickens novel. I dump my car in the no parking zone out front and throw the door open. I wish I'd listened to Mel's advice about keeping a revolver in my glovebox for just such a situation as this.

My muffler clatters onto the pavement as I sprint past a boarded-up townhouse. The seductive signage of the Electric Sewer lures me like a moth to a flame. A vixen outlined in neon works the pole, gracefully bending over and then wagging her finger 'come hither' at me. As the unmistakable roar of a V-8 at full throttle echoes in the distance, I slip the doorman a few bills to make cover and duck inside.

The main dance floor is located down the center of what was once a grand entryway, its crystal chandeliers now thick with cobwebs. The walls were at some point hastily rattle-canned an inoffensive shade of black, but patches of the old maroon paint are still evident in spots. I stare wistfully at the glimmering lights for a moment before I duck down one of the side passages. I intended to come here to blow some steam off and make a little love. Now I'm running from a psycho who probably wants to turn my pelt into a new pair of boots after literally fucking my eyes out. An infectious and electric Eurobeat groove drowns out any ambient noise as I stumble down the dimly lit corridor. I can't make out if I'm being followed over the thump of the bass. The air is stale and reeks of musk and cigarette smoke, and after a few minutes of it, I'm forced to lean against a doorframe as I double over with a coughing fit.

"Ah, Mr. Eubanks. What a pleasure." My eyes flick upward as I hack into my fist. A tiger with a wicked scar running across his throat stands in the middle of the hall. He grins at me with a chip tooth smile, but there's nothing behind his eyes. It's the look of a middle manager wistfully staring at a perfectly prepared cut of medium-rare tenderloin while the CEO makes a rambling speech about the importance of synergy. "I took the side entrance. You should try it some time."

"Who sent you?" I back away, but the tiger matches me pace-for-pace, keeping me within an arm's length.

"Does it really matter?" His claws extend, each one as big as a steak knife. They're covered with a dark sticky substance I realize is probably the blood of one of the Electric Sewer's security staff. "I'm going to soak this carpet with your blood in a moment, and then have my way with your corpse in the middle of the hallway. Will the miniscule bit of knowledge about who arranged for your demise make you feel any better about your predicament?"

"I probably can't match what they're paying you, but the Prosecutor's Office can do you one better. How does full immunity sound? All you have to do is go back down that hallway, and we can pretend like none of this ever happened." I do my best to fake a veneer of confidence, but the tiger sees through me like a pane of glass.

"No, I don't think so Mr. Eubanks. This is a matter of both business...and pleasure." The tiger drops his right paw down to his tight leather pants. *Zip*. The gleaming chrome zipper slides menacingly down, revealing the tip of his striped sheath. He gently slides it out into his paw, teasing his sheath as he blithely swipes his claws just inches from my jugular. Just as his spine-covered head emerges from that striped sheath, the door between us flies open, smacking him full force in the muzzle. A male couple–a buck and a cougar–slide out, muzzle against muzzle, paws down each other's tracksuit pants. Too busy going for round two in the hallway, they're apparently unaware of the perilous position they've placed themselves in. There's an aggrieved grunt and then the door swings in the opposite direction with double force, effortlessly sending them both sprawling to the ground.

"What's your damage man?" The cougar picks himself up and bares his fangs, his ears folding close against his headfur as his eyes dart between us. "You and your boyfriend couldn't wait an extra five seconds?"

I raise my paws, backing away. "Don't drag me into this. I'm just gonna bounce–"

Before I can finish my sentence, the tiger effortlessly grabs the cougar by the neck and lifts him off the floor. As the cougar desperately thrashes about, all my eyes can focus on is the tiger's arousal, his sizable cock emerging from his clenched paw. He gently strokes up and down his shaft as a steady trickle of blood stains the grungy carpet.

The buck's eyes aren't on me anymore, they're locked on the

tiger. I can smell the fear radiating from him. The buck's pheromones send a tingle running down my spine, activating the ancient part of my brain that once salivated at the thought of a juicy snow hare dashing across the frozen tundra. My own jeans suddenly feel uncomfortably tight.

The tiger squeezes harder. The cougar goes limp. The tiger's paw moves quickly, his predatory musk overpowering in a cramped space. The buck finally snaps. He makes it a few bounds before the tiger sinks his claws into the meat of his thigh. Bone loudly snaps as he tumbles to the floor.

"Help...me." The buck gasps, tears of agony beading on his cheeks as the tiger reels him in like a veteran fisherman.

"Isn't it erotic? There's nothing like the scent of fear to really get the blood pumping." The tiger casually tosses the cougar's body to the floor like a cub after spotting a new plaything. He grasps the buck by the throat, returning to stroking his cock with a blood-soaked paw. His eyes, a haunting shade of ghostly blue, stare emptily at me, a hint of a cruel smile on his lips. "I know you can smell it. You're just like me, a predator."

The buck uses the last of his strength to kick the tiger square in the sac. For a brief moment startled anger darts across the tiger's face. His paw tightens, crushing the buck's throat like an aluminum soda can. "Pity. I wanted to enjoy him a little longer." He pauses. "Perhaps I can."

There's a sickening, wet noise as the tiger uses his claws to separate the buck's head from his body. It only takes a moment for those deadly blades to cleanly slice through delicate connective tissue. The tiger stares at his prize for a moment before lowering it onto his erect, throbbing shaft. He uses the buck's tongue to lubricate himself up before sliding his cock inside the muzzle. Holding it firmly closed, he starts thrusting into it, bits of viscera splattering against the wall. He closes his eyes, panting as the buck's eyes stare at his navel. I could swear I see the buck blink just as I look away in disgust.

"I'll give you until I finish to hide, Mr. Eubanks. Please use your few remaining moments to contemplate which one of your orifices you'd like me to fuck after I terminate your existence." The tiger closes his eyes and starts violently thrusting his hips. I don't have long. "I eagerly await your response."

Something in me wants to stay and watch, like rubbernecking at the scene of a particularly gruesome car accident. After a moment, another part of me finally musters the courage to turn and get the hell out of there. I sprint past the tiger as fast as my bookish body can manage, skidding on a patch of bright red blood pooling on the floor. I manage to catch my balance as some of the blood soaks through my shoes. As I turn the corner, I hear loud chuffs of contentment, and an ominous *zip*.

Fuck.

Thank God my little circuit of the back corridors has led me straight back to the dance floor. As I enter the main part of the venue, the music becomes deafeningly loud. The lighting quickly disorients me, flash bulbs popping at random. A disco ball left over from the exuberant 70s shines yet more gleaming white light onto the dance floor. I'm half-blind as I scramble out of the hookup rooms and get into public space. A sinister pink rat watches from the bar, wiping down the counter with a tired rag. I debate on ordering a drink, but the bar is a good ten feet from the dance floor. I'd be too exposed there.

A warm body bumping against me brings me back to reality. The drugged-up crowd jostles around the dance floor in various stages of undress, testing for sexual prowess by observing each other's moves. The scent of musk is heavy in the air, and I gasp for a breath of fresh air as I feel like I'm drowning in a sea of leather and fur. Above the crowd, topless dancers gyrate and groove on sparkling platforms without a care in the world.

"You...lookin' for someone?" A lithe snow leopard in a mesh shirt and leather chaps places a comforting paw on my shoulder. He's about a foot taller than me. His piercing sea-green eyes, unusual for his species, light up with interest as they scan me over. His fangs glint like diamonds in the manic lighting of the dance floor. "You look lost, cub."

My mind ticks at a mile a minute before I make a snap judgment call. "Yeah, I'm lost. Do you think you could help me...find my way, daddy?"

I see the tiger emerging from the hallway in the corner of my vision. He's licking his paws clean. The snow leopard tucks me against him, wrapping his arm around my shoulder and gently squeezing my ass. I need to get out of here, now. Time to work the charm I usually keep in reserve for closing statements to the jury. I run a paw down his abs, so firm they could have been chiseled from marble by Michelangelo himself. I shoot him a million-dollar smile that says I'm down for anything. The snow leopard studies me for a moment, and then returns it. "Yeah. C'mon, let's go somewhere a little quieter. You look like you could use a little fun."

With his protective arm around me, I can't help but bury my muzzle into his thick chest fluff. My body language accentuates my submissiveness, my ears folded and my tail tucked against my leg. I shut my eyelids tight as my mind's eye pictures the tiger casually coming up from behind and turning me into shish kabob. I read somewhere that the brain stays conscious for a few moments after beheading. I don't want the last thing I see in this world to be the tiger's precum-covered cock slowly heading towards my muzzle.

Fortunately, we walk unmolested off the dance floor. I don't open my eyes until the electric groove in the background is disrupted by the creaking of a door. I take a few more steps inside. It clicks shut. The world becomes quieter here. The snow leopard's muzzle gently presses against mine. His lips taste like strawberries. "What's your name, cub?"

"Jack." His paws gently work at my fly. My jeans slide to the floor. The play room is dingy, but there's a double bed and a variety of questionable lubricants left behind by prior users piled on the bedside table.

"I'm Zale," he says, gently sliding my red silk boxers down. I'm surprised to see the tip of my cock is peeking out of my sheath. Zale gently massages my head with soft pawpads until I feel a surge of blood summon forth my delicate pink shaft. Zale's pawpads are like freshly tanned leather, and I can't help but let out a vulpine purr as he works me to full mast. The hormones coursing through my veins heighten the response, making me feel small and vulnerable. I'm sure Zale can sense it too. He assumes a dominant posture, taking control of my arousal.

It doesn't take long in Zale's confident paws for my cock to be ready for action. He gives my knot a playful squeeze before guiding me to brace myself on the bed. I whine with need, thumping my cock against the threadbare sheets.

"Shh, we're almost there." Zale squirts a generous dollop of lube from a purple tube onto his index pawpads and rubs them together. "Tail up for me, cub."

I dutifully comply, and a moment later, I feel Zale gently brush against my tailhole. "Before I do any exploring, have you cleaned yourself out?"

I look back over my shoulder and nod, blushing. Zale grins warmly at me. "Good work! Someone deserves a special treat for being so well prepared." His index finger gently presses under my tail, slickening me up. He's gentle but not too gentle, pitter-pattering his pawpads along my shaft to keep me excited. In the distance, I hear what sounds like wood splintering.

A few moments later, the pressure on my tailhole increases. I give a gentle push with my abdominal muscles to help him inside. He gradually stretches me with his index fingers, preparing me for what's to come. A cold dollop of lube squirts directly on my tailhole. I yelp, but the sensation sends a pleasing shiver down my spine. My fear mixes with desire, and I eagerly whine with lust.

Once Zale is satisfied that I'm slicked-up enough, he squirts a little more gel onto his erect cock, slathering his member until it glistens in the harsh, incandescent light. It's a handsome item, with little barbs that protrude from the head and shaft. It gently pulses with his relaxed heartbeat.

Zale leans over me, gently directing me into the proper position. I melt as his tongue runs across the nape of my neck. His paw firmly grasps my knot as I sense the pressure against my tailhole. I exhale a quiet grunt as he gently slides inside me, his paw teasing my shaft. A high-pitched noise cuts through the bass that permeates the club, but it's too jumbled to clearly make out. It could be the DJ fucking around on the turntables again.

The pressure takes a moment to build as Zale works his way in. He tightly grips my hips, his lube-covered penile spines providing another layer of stimulation as he slides inside me. Once the pressure reaches its apex, I assume Zale is as deep as he's going to get. He's bigger than I'm used to, but it feels like heaven, his shaft filling me with pulsating warmth. Zale softly moans as I clench around his cock for a moment and then release. A little drop of my pre dribbles onto the sheets, adding to the mess of what I assume are many others.

Zale pulls back, and the sensation of his lubricated barbs sliding through my tailhole is like being fucked with a puffer toy. I grip the far end of the mattress tight. Zale is zoned out in bliss, his eyes shut. He slides in and out of me like a pleasure automaton, alternating between running up my cock with his pawpads and down my cock with the gloriously soft winter coat fur on the back of his paws.

There's another sharp noise, distinctly like the sound flesh makes when slammed against drywall. My heart starts pumping faster. "Z-Zale?"

The snow leopard is too focused on filling me up to hear my nervous exclamation. He thrusts harder now, pounding me against the mattress, his paw now rapidly stroking my shaft. I whine and flatten my ears as the pressure slowly builds in my tip. It's the electric tingle that tells me I'm about to make a sticky mess of myself.

I hold my breath and focus on being in this moment. The fear is coursing through my veins and my heart is beating like I've been cold called on my first day of law school. The tiger is coming for me, I know it. I just want one fucking orgasm before he rips my throat out. Zale's musk hangs heavy in the air, his intoxicating arousal forcing me to bite my lip to avoid exploding then and there. I wait for his signal, overwhelmed by the rush of pleasure racing up my spine, desperate for a release.

Zale slaps my ass hard and then takes his paw away, pumping me a few more times with all his strength before I feel his warmth explode inside me. I groan and release, shooting a sticky rope onto my stomach fur. My cock empties the rest of its load onto the bed as Zale grips me tight, making sure not to slide out until he's filled me up fully with his seed. I deflate onto the bed, my mind briefly at peace, clouded by the orgasmic afterglow. My cheeks burn hot. My tongue lolls out as my muzzle rests on the mattress.

Crack. The door flies open and the doorknob embeds itself in the nightstand. The tiger stands in the doorway, his codpiece unzipped and his cock already dripping with pre. "Mr. Eubanks, I'm so glad you've decided to get one last fuck before I kill you." He casually picks at his bloodied teeth with his claws. "It's always good to go out on a high note."

Zale pivots to stand protectively in front of me. The tiger effortlessly bats aside Zale's right hook and grasps his sac in one of those monstrous paws. Zale howls in agony as the tiger squeezes. "Fascinating, isn't it? Just one little motion and you can reduce the fiercest creature to tears."

"Stop it! Please! You came here for me, not him." I sit up on the bed, clasping my paws together.

The tiger chuckles. "So I did." His paw clenches tight and Zale unleashes a raw, animalistic scream. His eyes roll back in his head, and he falls onto the bed foaming at the mouth. I look away from the bloodied mess only half covered by his pubic fur.

"Can you at least allow me to die with pants on? I don't want tomorrow's front page to be me sprawled on this bed with my cock out." I raise my paws to show I'm unarmed.

The tiger glances at his LCD calendar watch and shrugs. "I scheduled this until midnight. Be my guest."

I slowly slip my jeans on, the soft Italian fabric sliding over my fur. Right leg, then left. My paws shake with such intensity I can't make out the numbers on my Swatch. My vison narrows until it's just me and him, his cold eyes scanning me over like a machine, calculating where to cut to optimize exsanguination. His eyes briefly flit downward, perhaps pondering the novelty of slashing my femoral artery, but then his eyes dart upward and lock with mine. Ah, he plans to go with the old standby of slashing the carotid. Joy.

Seconds seem like hours as I struggle to fasten the waistband. He could just kill me right now. He's toying with me, allowing me the pleasure of breathing these last few breaths, letting me enjoy the sensation of soft denim on my pawpads for just a moment longer. Finally, after I feel like a second more of his eyes boring into my skull would drive me to madness, I settle with zipping it up, leaving the top button loose.

"Have you decided on a hole?" It's all come down to this. No escape, no running. Just me and a cold, unfeeling killing machine in a cramped, windowless room. I lower my arms, watching as those pearlescent claws spring forth from their sheath. I close my eyes and take a deep breath, the metallic reek of blood clogging my nostrils.

"My ass, if you'd be so kind. It's already been warmed up for you." It'll all be over soon. Just a little cut.

"An excellent choice." There's a sudden yelp of surprise. My eyes spring open. The tiger staggers forward, eyes wide open in shock. *Cha chock. Crack.* He looks down at the gaping hole where his pubic mound was a moment ago. The tiger stoically examines himself for a moment before collapsing to his knees. He attempts to take a deep breath, but he's like a fish flapping on dry sand now. Eyes still locked on me until the very end, he exhales and then silently keels over.

Melissa is on bended knee in the doorway, licking a mixture of blood and shit off the end of the sawed-off shotgun. Her delicate tongue on the gun barrel reminds me of a Caravan album I used to listen to in high school. For just a moment a look in her eyes reminds me of the tiger. I blink and then it's gone.

"Did...did you just shoot him up the ass?"

Melissa casually tucks the firearm back into a black leather holster on her hip. "We all have our kinks, John. Don't think too hard about it."

I take a deep breath and pretend I didn't hear that. After a moment, my paws stop shaking enough that I find I can fasten the button on my jeans. "You think the barman has a phone? We should probably call C.S.U. and let them handle the cleanup." I look over at the bed. Zale is still breathing, but I don't think he'll be filling anyone else for the foreseeable future. Pity. "And we need to call a bus for the victim here."

Mel nods. "I thought I saw a phone over by the Southern Comfort, along with a sign for 2-for-1 Alabama Slammers. Let's get it called in and then drinks are on me. It's the least I can do." She zips up her multicolor windbreaker to conceal the weapon and slicks her heavily gelled headfur back. "Let's go enjoy the electric groove and sort this out all on Monday."

I look at the trail of destruction outside and feel the tiniest pang of arousal stir within me.

"Yeah. We can sort it out on Monday."

A FAT JACKRABBIT AND OTHER BARGAIN ODDITIES BASED ON A TRUE STORY

NIKKOLAS JAMES

Lonnie's dick was useless. A rabbit with a useless dick was like a therapy dog with rabies—a complete incapability of fulfilling your natural purpose. And purpose doesn't stop. It continues all around you. John stood in Lonnie's cubicle at least once a week and unfurled the pictures of his children stacked in his wallet. All Lonnie could see was a long, plastic-tongued testament to John's substantial cock reaching all the way down to the carpet, no pun intended. All in Lonnie's face, at least once a week. The picture sleeves were full on both sides with different kids. Lonnie was always polite. Being polite was about all he had left. If he was impotent *and* an asshole, then everyone would say he deserved the impotence. Lonnie never discussed it with anyone, at least not at work, but he was old enough now that any rabbit would know, and anyone else who knew about rabbits, which was everyone. Lonnie was convinced that half the reason John always stopped by was because he was under the impression that his virility might rub off on him. John was one of those rabbits that believed everything was just a matter of having a positive mental attitude. That and wheatgrass. He'd bring wheatgrass to Lonnie and they'd do shots of it together. Lonnie thought it tasted like an old soggy haybale miraculously shit a freshly mowed lawn. But again. Polite.

Not everyone at work was polite. Lonnie's boss, Ted, a porcupine and Lonnie's cousin through marriage, thought he was a loser. He never said it. But he would say things like "Lonnie! Only moping, whiny *hop-alongs* dye their ears black!" in front of everyone. Marsha, Frank, Tom, and Vicki—hyenas, would always snicker. It was a small staff in a small office. There was no getting away from them. When Lonnie would go to the breakroom for a snack, Frank would whisper *hop-along* under his breath, and the other three would snicker some more. Lonnie got to where he'd keep his Walkman clipped to his front pants pocket and headphones on as much as possible. The day he came in with his ears dyed pink, he kept Bonanza Banzai's *1984* playing all day long so he wouldn't have to hear the sneers and judgments. Even when John came by, he acted like he didn't hear him, even though by that time the batteries in his Walkman had died. John finally went away.

Lonnie was the "computer guy" in the office. Issues rarely came up, and when they did, they were quick and easy to fix. John regularly needed his computer cleared of viruses due to an almost inconceivable porn addiction. Even with all the fucking he did at home, Lonnie thought. That's one unstoppable cock. Lonnie figgered the more specific the porn, the more serious the disease. By that summer, John had drilled down, no pun intended, to *bound bukkake hentai scream.* It was porn that didn't even exist—the hundreds of pictures were artist renderings. Several of them starring a cartoon hermaphroditic samurai badger. Lonnie always quietly cleaned it up as a favor. And out of respect. Other times, when Lonnie needed to look busy, like when Ted made his hourly rounds, he would endlessly reformat the same pile of floppy disks. Once Ted was out of sight, he'd continue playing *Doom 2* or *Baldur's Gate.* Usually, on breaks, Lonnie would still just sit at his desk and look up at the lights. Something about the fluorescent lights, so close to the neon of The Electric Sewer, Lonnie would sit and stare into them—listen to them hum and imagine he was standing in line outside the sewer instead. In those moments, it was always Friday night. The only thing better was when it was actually Friday night.

"Maybe we should get our dicks pierced?" Ernie said. Ernie was a chinchilla and Lonnie's best friend. Most chinchillas are gray and black with beady black eyes. Ernie was mosaic, a.k.a. a "fancy" chinchilla. His colors were silver and white, and his eyes looked black but they were actually blue. That dark of blue. Light had to hit them for you to tell, and standing outside the sewer with the neon hitting them, they looked like an ocean storm on fire. Everyone hit on Ernie. But he hated to be touched. Chinchillas have notoriously soft and fluffy fur. Like petting a cloud. To mitigate the compulsion in other people to therefore pet him, Ernie moussed his fur into long spikes all over his body and dyed them purple and black. It was an issue from time to time. Going through a turnstile or a revolving door. Riding in a car, Ernie had to sit way forward in the seat and hold onto the dash. They were on their way to The Electric Sewer. Lonnie drove a '96 Mercury Sable LS, reliable, nothing too whacky, other than the fact that it was painted with a mural of an ogre being fellated by the snake heads of Medusa. And Medusa's actual head had a really bored look on its face. It was a birthday gift from Ernie. He unveiled it in Lonnie's office parking lot. Lonnie had to have a meeting with HR after.

"Pierced?!" Lonnie said. He had to turn down the Cosmicity to make sure he was hearing right.

"Yeah!" Ernie said. "You know. Why not? Maybe that's the ticket. Release some pressure from it and then *boom*, ol' hickory."

Lonnie laughed. Ernie was the only person he ever told about his impotence, and Ernie, like most people you'd find at the sewer, completely accepted that about him, didn't snicker or sneer, and any humor around it was good-natured and designed to make Lonnie feel better about himself.

"Who is going to pierce our dicks?" Lonnie said.

"There's gotta be a porcupine at the sewer who'd be interested in a dare."

Lonnie laughed harder.

They pulled up to the club and got a parking spot right in front, which almost never happened. Lonnie felt like it was a sign. They were about to have a great night. The kind that changed lives. As they stood in line, that feeling only got stronger for Lonnie. Someone was blasting Kissing the Pink out of a Trans-Am, on the hood of which a tangle of four pussycats were taking the music quite literally. Mewling. Sixty-nine intertwined. It was called "furballing." Something so sewer-normal they may as well have been splitting milkshakes and fries. Everyone else in line was at least bobbing their head along to the music, if not outright dancing. Lonnie wasn't much of a dancer, but he loved the joy it brought to the people around him. He flopped his ears down, clenched his eyes shut, and basked in the heat of the red neon sign—The Electric Sewer. That's when Lonnie smelled it. Food. But not like any food he'd ever smelled before in his life. Instantly made his mouth water. He kept his eyes shut and let his nose lead him out of line. His whiskers were twitching like crazy. When Lonnie finally opened his eyes, he saw it—a food truck sitting at the back of the parking lot. He walked toward it.

The truck was white with bright red lettering. It looked like an ice cream truck but bigger. The light inside where the proprietor paced back and forth was bright blue. It even had a humming white neon sign on the roof casting a welcoming glare on the red leather barstools welded to the side. Lonnie read the name out loud: "The Nonstop Truckstop."

Lonnie looked at the raccoon standing inside wearing a black and yellow leather luchador mask and matching speedo. The speedo was big enough to fit "Eat Me" across the crotch. Lonnie pointed up at the sign. "I get it," he said. "Because you're always stopped?" The raccoon stared at him. "As in parked?" Lonnie said.

The raccoon clicked his tongue against his teeth. "You got it," he said.

Lonnie sat down on a stool and took a deep whiff of whatever was cooking inside. He looked around for a menu and didn't see one. He looked around inside the truck for a menu board. There wasn't one.

"Menu?" Lonnie asked.

"I know what you're here for," the raccoon said. A chill ran up Lonnie's spine all the way to the tops of his ears. He shivered.

"Um, I guess, one, then, please?" he said.

The raccoon uncrossed his arms and started to move to the row of hooded steam trays behind him. A hand slapped on Lonnie's shoulder. He jumped and almost fell off the stool.

"Dude!" Ernie said. "What are you doing? We're almost inside. Food comes *after* we're drunk, remember? S'go." Ernie more or less had to pull Lonnie off the stool and away from the truck. Lonnie watched the raccoon quietly return to his standing spot and cross his arms. He looked frantically up and down the truck for business hours but didn't see any. If Lonnie weren't so polite, he would have punched Ernie in the face and raced right back to that stool. But he was. And besides, who punches their best friend over food truck food?

Inside, the club was hot and crowded. Lonnie thought, has it always smelled like this? He cupped his hands over his nose and sniffed up the residue of the food truck smell. When that was gone, his T-shirt still had some left, so he put the collar of it over his nose. When all of it was all gone, he screamed at Ernie over the Depeche Mode that he was going to get them some drinks. Really, the last thing he wanted to talk to the bartender about was drinks. It took forever to get Carlos's attention, and he wasn't much help.

"What do you know about the food truck parked outside?" Lonnie asked.

Carlos said, "I know it's a food truck and that it's parked outside."

"But did the owner come in here and ask if he could park his food truck in your lot?"

"Of course he did."

"What did he say?"

"He asked if he could park his food truck in my lot."

Lonnie gave up and ordered a double rye whiskey, neat. Ernie asked where his drink was when Lonnie caught back up with him. Lonnie handed him the whiskey. He didn't feel much like drinking anyway. His thoughts were solely on the food truck outside. But he didn't want to ditch Ernie. Every Friday night, for months now, they hung out together at The Electric Sewer. Start with drinks. Hit up the oxygen bar. Next was the dirty internet café where porn was not only allowed, it was encouraged. More drinks. Even more drinks. Figure-eight stumble down the street to the all-night doner kebab place, eat, rally, drive home, and pass out. Sometimes puke and then pass out. Even the chaos of their misery had a comfortable routine.

When Ernie immediately drained the double rye and asked for another, Lonnie hatched a plan. He went back to the bar, ordered more rye whiskey, this time in soda, but asked for a plain soda for himself. Over the next couple of hours, Lonnie planned to feed Ernie drink after drink after drink until he passed out. The plan was derailed at the oxygen bar. Ernie was already so drunk, before they even had the masks sanitized, he was fellating himself, which caught the attention and severely turned on a set of twin white mice sitting next to him. Of course, when they tried to go with it and join in, the instant one of them touched him, Ernie made his "grumpy noise"—a low, sharp groan. Lonnie reached over and petted the back of Ernie's head to get him to calm down. As far as Lonnie knew, he was the only person allowed to do that—to touch Ernie at all. The mice, sensing the connection, got even more electric. They crawled over Ernie to Lonnie. Almost simultaneously, one tongue was in his mouth and another around his furry flaccid cock. Lonnie froze. In that moment, he prayed. Like trying to will a piece of shit car to start. Please, baby. *Please.* Every second that passed was agony. It was hopeless. He was a wet egg noodle dropped on the kitchen floor and kicked against a baseboard. The mouse finally gave up, reached for the oxygen mask, and said, "Maybe we can blow it up, baby?" Her sister stopped kissing Lonnie and looked and then they both erupted into laughter. Lonnie looked over at Ernie. Ernie was passed out. Lonnie shoved the girls off him, wiped the hot, humiliated tears out of his eyes, and bolted outside. The truck was still there. The stools were still empty. Lonnie practically ran himself into the side of the truck getting back to the stool. The raccoon stared at him, chewing on a toothpick.

"One?" he asked.

Lonnie nodded vigorously. The raccoon turned, opened a steam tray, and ladled hot food into a large bowl. He set the bowl in front of Lonnie. It was meat in a brown gravy. Lonnie stuck his nose over the steam and sucked in harder than at an oxygen bar. It was perfectly seasoned, and when he poked the meat with a fork, it fell apart right into the gravy. Lonnie drooled. The raccoon set an ice-cold jar of pickled carrots and a pair of small metal tongs on the counter next to the bowl. Lonnie almost made himself choke. He definitely burned his tongue. He shoveled the food in his mouth as fast he could. The cold tang of the carrots chased the savory meat around the flavor playground in his mouth, and the game of tag continued even when he gulped it down into his stomach. The ball of food sat front and center and hummed like a warm neon sun.

Then, it happened. His dick moved. Lonnie dropped his fork. It bounced off the bowl and clattered across the counter. The raccoon, cleaning a knife, turned around and looked at Lonnie.

"You okay, buddy?" he asked.

Lonnie nodded, reached his hands down into his lap, and felt. It moved again. He almost jumped off the stool. Slowly, he picked his fork back up and continued eating. His dick kept moving. By the time he had the bowl to his lips slurping up the gravy, he was at half-mast. If the raccoon hadn't been staring at him, he would have licked the bowl clean.

"Another, please?" Lonnie said.

The raccoon shook his head. "One is enough," he said.

Lonnie's ears instantly fell and slapped him on the back. He pulled his wallet out of his pocket so fast he nearly threw it at the racoon. There were no pictures of kids in Lonnie's wallet, so that meant there was plenty of money. He spilled it across the counter.

"I don't care what I have to pay," Lonnie said.

The raccoon snorted. "That ain't it," he said.

Completely forgetting himself, Lonnie reached across the

counter and grabbed a handful of the raccoon's chest fur. Lonnie let him go almost immediately and began to profusely apologize. "I'm so sorry," he said. "I can't really explain, but your food...let's just say I think it's fixing something that's broken inside of me and I *really* want more, please, um, what's your name?"

The racoon smoothed out the ruffled fur on his chest. "Ralph," he said.

"Ralph, is there *anything* I can do? Did you run out of something I could fetch from the supermarket? Do you need some dishes done first? Anything?"

Ralph said, "The ingredients I need ain't at no supermarket. Relax, kid. I'll be back next week. You can have some more then."

Lonnie felt the terror of having to wait even another minute drain the color out of his entire body. He knew that if he continued to argue or make a scene, the prospect of eating the food again would be even further away, if not eliminated completely. He got up, thanked Ralph, paid, and left a huge tip, no pun intended. But Lonnie hadn't exactly given up. It turned out, there in fact was a porcupine in the sewer interested in a dare. Lonnie didn't even have to pay him. He just had to tell him the food truck outside wasn't using locally sourced ingredients. As the porcupine headed outside, Lonnie scooped Ernie up and helped him out to the car. Ernie spilled into the backseat and passed back out.

Lonnie turned around and walked back toward the food truck. He watched the porcupine disappear behind the truck and a second later, there was a loud pop and hiss, and the truck lurched to the left, shaking everything inside. The porcupine ran down the street screaming, "Fuck global, support local!" Cussing, Ralph flung the truck's back doors open and gave chase for a bit. When he did, Lonnie snuck in through the open back doors and found a place to hide behind a stack of produce boxes. Over the next hour, Lonnie listened, first to Ralph call for a repair. Then, out the window, he watched the sewer let out and a group of three drunk punks figure-eight their way over to the food truck. Lonnie watched Ralph serve them. He could smell the food. It wasn't what Ralph had served him. Not even close. It still smelled *good* and the customers greedily devoured it, but Lonnie had been that drunk lots of times. One night, his doner kabab had a cockroach in it, and he just picked it off like a pickle he didn't want and dove right in. A mechanic showed up to change the tire. When that was done, the customers left, and Ralph closed up shop.

Lonnie didn't really have a plan. He realized that after maybe five minutes of hiding behind the boxes. He figgered Ralph would drive home and leave him in the truck. Then, he could rifle through and maybe find a recipe? Or leftovers? Lonnie didn't know. What he did know was he felt closer to big naming his cock than he'd ever felt before. *Dick–rod–wang–Shaft–Mr. Spelman–The Box Cutter.* He felt like he had a chance at another life.

As the truck bumped along, Lonnie, still full, was almost lulled to sleep. The only thing that kept him awake was at one point, the truck slowed down substantially. It was just inching along. Carefully, Lonnie reached over, slid the window next to him open, and poked his head out. The truck was shambling down an alley with the headlights off. Lonnie looked further down, and one of the customers that had eaten earlier, a skunk in a leather jacket, was drunkenly bouncing his way down the alley. Suddenly, fury kicked into the engines, and the truck bolted down the alley toward the skunk. Lonnie wouldn't have even had time to warn him. Lonnie pulled his head back inside park and got up. Lonnie scrambled to his butt and backed away from Ralph advancing. Ralph stopped at the counter, picked up a huge butcher knife, and scraped Lonnie off the floor. Lonnie couldn't believe how strong the raccoon was. Lonnie's back was against the wall, and his feet weren't touching the floor.

"You just *had* to see how the sausage was made, huh?" Ralph said, putting the tip of the butcher knife against Lonnie's ribs. Lonnie didn't know a lot about anatomy but somehow, he knew with one good thrust, Ralph would have that knife in his heart.

Lonnie squeezed his eyes shut and shouted, "*PLEASE!* I *need* your food. What did this guy do? Not tip? I get it. Fuck him. I won't tell anyone. I can't eat here if you're in jail."

The knife went away from Lonnie's chest and his feet were gently set back down on the floor. Lonnie slowly opened his eyes and saw Ralph staring inquisitively at him.

"I gotta say," Ralph said. "No one's *ever* liked my cooking that much. What is it, kid? Something your mommy used to make back when she was alive?"

"My mother's still alive," Lonnie said. "She lives in Oklahoma City."

"So, what is it then?"

"It makes my dick hard, okay?" Lonnie didn't see any sense in lying. "It's been a problem my whole life. I've been to medical doctors, therapists, nutritionists, herbalists, acupuncturists. A fucking fortune teller, once. Nothing's worked. Until tonight. And it was your food. Do you have *any* idea what it's like being a rabbit without a family?" Lonnie was almost crying. "If society were more honest about itself, they would've put a bullet in the back of my head a long time ago." He was interrupted by a sound outside. Like something would scream if it could get enough air. The run over skunk. Lonnie looked over at the window. "Oh, Jesus as a gopher..." he said.

Unblinking, Ralph stuck his head out to take a look. Then, he went and threw the back doors of the truck open. Bathed in the lambent red of the truck's taillights, the skunk lay in the street broken in half, swimming in a pool of blood. His trying to scream came out in loud, yawning moans. Ralph opened a small closet next to the grill.

"Fender tenderizin' is the best," he said. "But it don't always get the job done. You know, I wouldn't have to do this if the quality of beef in this country hadn't gone to shit over the last twenty years. Might as well wrap tires in butcher paper and pass them out. You ask me, part of it was when we stopped using the right tools for the job." He reached into the closet and pulled out a sledgehammer. He looked at Lonnie. "If you want more food, flaccid McGee," he said, "then you better get to work." He handed Lonnie the sledgehammer.

Lonnie took it, laid it on the floor, hopped out of the truck, and dragged the hammer out after him. Slowly, he went over to the skunk. The skunk wasn't making noise anymore, but he was moving, or writhing or whatever, so Lonnie knew he was still alive. Lonnie hesitated until the smell hit him. You know how skunks are supposed to smell, especially when they get run over. But there was none of that. All Lonnie could smell, even leaning down over the skunk, was that piping hot meat and gravy. It was like the skunk bathed in it. Lonnie's cock was immediately back on the job and once Lonnie, mouth watering, lifted the hammer up and brought it down on the skunk's head with a loud *CRACK!* his dick was harder than advanced calculus. He kept swinging until he was cracking concrete.

"Well well well," Ralph said, watching from up in the truck. "Table for one, Mr. Spelman?" Ralph laughed, and Lonnie, out of breath, laughed like the skunk had tried to scream and kept laughing once his air was back and he could breathe again. And when he could breathe again, it was like being born and breathing for the very first time. Lonnie felt all the life behind it as he reached down, dipped a finger in, and tasted it. The current that ran through his body pulled him to his knees. He crawled over the body, his hands and feet slipped deep into the pools of blood. Lonnie found a hole. Made of leather, made of death, made of metal, made of flesh, he wasn't sure, and it didn't matter. As he began to thrust, he looked up at Ralph. Ralph had a sketchpad open and a pen in his hand–laughing again and drawing furiously.

THE JACK

CEDRIC G! BACON

If you wanna know the real story and not some secondhand bunch of bullshit, I'm the one you wanna talk to, Tommy DeCarlo, and lemme just say if it wasn't for me none of this would've happened.

When I was growing up there was only one of three ways a beagle like me could've gotten out of the old neighborhood: You could join a street crew and get a bullet in your head. You could join the military and do your time and try and be a hero...and get a bullet in your head.

Or you could do what I did and use what you got to get out. That means you could be a singer, a brainy motherfucker and join a business in the city, or you use street sense and take it to the man to make a little extra cheese.

That's what I did.

And what's more, I did it all with no bullet in my head.

But that's not this story.

Here's the stone cold truth as only I can tell it.

"How you feel?" Carlos said to me, above the calm pour of the bottle's contents into two waiting glasses.

I looked at the back of Carlos' head, studying the rat's fat rolls and the scar just at the base of his skull. Benny once said that Becca said that's where he had a part of his brain cut out from a lover he pissed off and that Carlos kept that lover's dick pickled in a jar in his apartment.

But like I said, this is about a real story, not some made-up shit.

So I said back to Carlos, "What do you mean?"

"Few win against me," answered Carlos. He was strolling over to Benny now, who'd been strapped to the leather-padded board, the dalmatian's forelimbs spread high above his latex-encased head. His cock was a dark red inside the plastic casement, as the aluminum rings of the milking machine slid down on the shaft of his dick and the steady humming filled the silence. I listened to him wince in pain, again and again as it felt like the vacuum of the pump was about to rip his cock off his body.

"You never gave up," Carlos continued. "Great stamina and patience. Don't see that often."

I shrugged, but inside I was nervous as hell. "Wasn't nothing, really."

"It was something. I'm impressed. Good boy."

At this I couldn't help but wag my tail. It wasn't too often that the rat doled out accolades, but then again it wasn't often a guy like me found themselves this far in his backroom, the famous "House of Cards" that all the chicks and dudes on the outside of the Electric Sewer talked about. There were a lot of stories which filtered out, someone telling someone such and so-forth. But unless you got back here, you didn't know for sure if any of that was real or just really fake. Hell, even Benny would surely enjoy the fact that he was now part of the great shuffle of stories folks would say about the Electric Sewer.

Back here, all the neon lattices, the swirling colorful strobes that a canine like me can't quite see but, when I'm good and blitzed out, can feel myself swimming through that subliminal hum at a speed faster than light, all that falls to the wayside, and it's like walking through the dankest cave ever carved up. When I made that first long and sprawling walk from the main bar down to the House of Cards, all that haze kind of fell away and the music faded from boom-boom-boom four on the four beat into a low pulsating throb that when I put my paw to the walls felt like a thin and reedy heartbeat.

Unlike the other games, there was only one rule at Carlos' table, and that was that Carlos never lost.

Ever.

That's what Benny always said, at least. The dalmatian never really believed that it was possible for me to come in and beat Carlos' ass like he's never been beaten before. That was Benny all over, always doubting and always negative.

Things like that didn't happen often, or at least to anyone who lived to talk about it.

Benny didn't think things like that could happen.

But it could.

It did.

And I'm gonna tell you how.

"So the thing they always say about Carlos," Benny said, "is that he never loses."

It was already night when Benny and me crossed over from the Bed-Stuy onto Ludlow, where the Electric Sewer sat down at the end of the lane like some mountain. I mention this because if you've never crossed the Bed-Stuy onto Ludlow, then you don't know just how pitch black it can get when the streetlights are shot out. Benny was the only bright light I had to guide me—because he was a dalmatian, the ivory parts of his fur made him stand out more than the ebony spots down his neck and backside did.

"Bullshit," I said to him, with all the stubbornness of a

beagle as we walked inside. What can I say, it's an inborn flaw of mine. "How the hell do you figure that? Everyone loses." We crossed the long hallway before the music of Air Wolf hit us full-on in the face when we took our usual seats at the far end of the bar. Elric, the Electric Sewer's muscle and a bull no one wanted to mess with, walked around without even trying to blend in. He was tall and massively built, with a t-shirt four sizes too small that clung to his chest like a second skin, hooves stuffed into his pockets or folded across his chest, tension following him like a cloud of dust at his heels. Carlos, the bartender, didn't wave to us—but that was typical, and saying "hello" was a thing that wasn't his bag. His thing is to cock an eyebrow at anyone coming in as a greeting and then ignoring them until they wanted something.

Now I don't know the full history of the Electric Sewer—for all I know, when the world rose out of the slime and dinosaurs walked the ground it was probably here. You saw all ages around here, young, old, the really young and the really old, some trying to hold on to their lost youth and some trying to be all growed before their time. Benny and I had youth on our side, which sometimes helped us prey on the loneliness of the old fucks who sat drinking by themselves in the club and wouldn't mind having a couple of sweet young things to wile their hours away with. Plus it helped when we were strapped for cash and were in want of drinks to try and pick these pockets, all without having to slip our paws inside for their wallets, though sometimes gripping their dicks made them be temp sugar daddies a lot faster.

My card-playing brought in some money, but the quickest way for a buck was to be doted on by someone, especially in this place where if you dressed about as demure—big word, I know—as possible, you were likely to get one of these old fucks' attention. They tended to like Benny more; it was something about being a skinnily built dalmatian with big innocent eyes that lured them in. Me, who was about the same build and size as Benny, must've let off a more threatening air, or they figured I didn't look anywhere near as innocent or naive as Benny did. But it was whatever, if they wanted Benny I let them have him—Benny knew the deal, and when it was over with we had a little more money to go out drinking with.

This night, Benny shook his head, ears flopping against his skull as he disagreed with my plan to earn a little more money than the piddly stuff we'd been getting. "Nah, man, I'm serious. I heard it from Becca who—"

"And how'd she hear it?"

"I was getting there, if you'd just let me. She was serving drinks back there, right there, and was watching it, getting in close enough to see everyone's paws."

"And what'd she see?"

"Carlos wasn't about to lose. He didn't lose his cool, and he kept raising the stakes til everyone folded and he won."

"So everyone gave up thinking he had a shit-hot paw but didn't."

"Basically," Benny said.

"That's poker for you, Ben," I explained. "It's all about the odds and bluffing yourself into being a badass. Everyone eventually loses if you're not paying attention."

Benny sighed caustically and said, "But not you, Tommy. Ain't that right?"

I grinned in reply. I didn't wanna seem, you know, ubiquitous—but it was true. I never lost. I flashed a well-worn deck out from my shirt sleeve and rolled a claw over the edges, loving the crisp, crackling sound of the cards flapping against one another more than the song blasting over the club's speakers. This was music to my ears, sweeter than honey from a bee or the pouring of wine over rocks in a glass.

Shuffling the deck, I say to Benny, "Call it."

"When," Benny says as I stop and hold up the card he'd paused me on.

"Alright, study it good." I cut the deck, shuffled a couple times, and said, "Let me tell you something Benny, you got to have faith when it comes to all this. None of that wimpy, worrying stuff you're always nagging me over."

Benny frowned. "I nag because I think you take too many risks. Being cuddled and sucking someone off who's lonely is one thing, but this is dangerous."

I didn't wanna say he was wrong. Sure, making a living the way I did meant I'd probably lose more than I won. That was just the nature of that beast. "But if I weren't taking risks we wouldn't have a roof over our heads. This your card?" I said, holding up the 3 of Hearts.

"I never get tired of your tricks," Benny said, and snuggled up next to me. But by his scent, I could see there was more, and I caught that vague whimper behind each word he spoke. "But come on, Tom, you seriously don't think you can take on Carlos?"

I shrugged. "Why not? Someone has to."

"I dunno..." Benny let this kind of hang in the air, like he was hoping they'd fall back down, get absorbed into me like osmosis.

I hated it when he'd do that. It annoyed me that he had these doubts because it hammered doubt into my mind. And any cardsharp will tell you, when you've got doubt you're gonna fuck up and get fucked up. "So what're you trying to say to me?" I said, shrugging him off.

"I think we should just pack this all in and start looking at regular jobs," he answers. "At least we won't have to worry about eating or taking a chance like we have been."

"You worry too much," I sighed. "Life wouldn't be interesting if we didn't take chances on anything. If we just played it safe, how would we learn what's on the other side of life's door?"

"What's that even supposed to mean?" asked Benny.

"Hell if I know." I lied, because I did know. Poker was the only god I trusted, even if it was all down to chance. Looking in the eyes of someone when you've totally destroyed their sense of pride and taken them for all they had isn't something you can have with a gun in your paws or a knife against your ribs. You can't kill your way back from embarrassment—a loss in a poker game is a loss that sticks with you for the rest of your worthless life. I lived for it, and my winnings kept me and Benny from having to sing or suck for our supper.

At the Electric Sewer, everyone was a personality: you had those who were dressed to the nines, in crushed velvet smoking jackets, top hats and tails like they stepped out of the nineteenth century. Some had the tips of their fur dyed in a lot of different hues. Some didn't have shirts on, only wearing their gold necklaces which thumped against bare torsos. The vixens spun and turned on their heels and partners dipped and twirled on the dance floor and came back to the bar huffing and puffing for a second wind.

I said we dressed demure—still a big word—and I mean it. Jeans, couple plaid shirts between us, sometimes a necktie for me like tonight and a flat cap laying sideways on my head. We got the scoffs from all the fancy-dressed who wanted to impress, but who were we impressing? Not them, that's for sure. Down at the edge of the bar was an old beaver who raised a toast towards Benny and I, leading me to sip on my drink and sigh while Benny returned the toast. Benny wanted to play nice, impress the guy a little bit maybe even comment on his pointed length if given the chance and accept the commentary on all of his spots. I wasn't about to stop him if the beaver was interested and Benny wanted that chump change.

Me, I was keen for something else and was scanning around until I found my opening. It was there, near a back corner half-hidden by the lid of the club, a table where three or four bodies lingered, ears twitching furtively and tails sloped over and flopping along their chairs. I was licking my lips like I was hungry and made the first moves to get up, when I felt Benny's tug at my forearm. "What is it?"

"I know you're not gonna listen to me," said Benny.

"You're right about that."

"But listen to me one more time before you go over there. Carlos never loses. If you're trying to get his attention, think about what's gonna happen if you get to play him."

"I'm gonna take him for all he's got," I said. "Nothing simpler than that."

"Tom, listen to me, I've heard some bad shit about Carlos when he does lose."

"I thought you said he doesn't."

"That we know of," Benny says, "but I've heard things. Bad things."

I shrugged this off. "What kinda bad shit could that old man be up to? All he does is run a bar and play some cards." I said it, but I didn't really believe it all that much. The story about the band-aid on the back of his head for one; the other was the portraits above the bar of what Carlos called his "favored guests." Folks who'd apparently earned his respect and that he wanted to keep around even if they didn't come around no more. It was always creepy the way the eyes shone whenever

Benny and me met those glimpses, almost like Carlos had put some kind of strobe inside.

If I was concerned about any of this, I didn't share it with Benny. I was kinda curious to see what would happen.

"Then if you're not gonna listen to me, listen to this: you remember Fuqua, right?" Benny said. "The iguana from the 42nd Street Razors?"

"Yeah," I answered, "but didn't he move away or something?" I knew his face too and looked back to the paintings where Carlos had one of the iguana holding a few cards and slyly smiling at the viewer, the eyes flickering under the neon lights.

Benny shook his head at this. "This is what Becca told me: he played Carlos at his table, and he bluffed his way into a winning pot."

"So he beat Carlos?" I asked, not believing him.

"Yeah he did, and he didn't ever come back out, or at least Becca didn't see him walk back out and none of the other Razors have seen him since."

"Are you sure a Pentagram didn't carve him up?" I joked, hoping to get a laugh out of Benny. He didn't grin and his face looked drawn as his jowls and flew drooped into a frown.

"I think Carlos killed him," he said, "because Fuqua beat him, and I bet Elric fucks his corpse every night."

"Alright, that's disgusting," I mused. "But come on, that can't even be true. How do you even know that? Becca again?"

"I'm just telling you what she tells me."

"And you believe her? Come on Ben, I thought you were smarter than that. Think about it: everyone loses. No one's invincible to it."

"Except you, right?" There was no humor behind Benny's words. I could see that worry flood his eyes, and I sighed again.

"Tommy, let's just pay for our drinks and get out of here. My mom told me about a couple gas station jobs down the Southside that got our names on them if we just apply."

"When the hell are you gonna trust me that I know what I'm doing? I know what's best for me and what's best for you. And what's more..." I said, making a grab for Benny's purse. Much to my shock, he had an iron-like grip on it, which contained all of the money we had in the world.

"Don't do this, Tommy," he sniffed, his hold weakening as I snatched harder at it. "Please, I'm begging you, something don't feel right about any of this."

"Will you relax?" I said, finally getting a hold on the purse. "I'll be back."

Once I got to the table, all their heads turned to me and their fur bristled. True I could've been a little more subtle about my intentions, but they didn't know me and I didn't know them; in the end it didn't matter who trusted who once I made it clear that I was here to play.

The main dealer, a wolf, nodded wary approval my way with his muzzle, and that was that. He was strongly built, with a silk vest that exposed his bare chest, which I admired for a moment. He wasn't much of my type and if I wasn't in a hurry to take his money I'd have complimented him on whatever workout routine he had. I briefly violated my own rules and lingered too long, getting his attention when he looked up and flexed. I grinned, the last bit of respect I was gonna show him, then sat down across from him. This was all part of the game, that art form to read folks' faces and knowing what their cards were gonna be by the way their eyes cut and rolled and lips licked along their maws. Some held their cards worse than their liquor, and them same maws gaped, like a whored-out asshole, when they're shocked that someone out-bluffed them.

I didn't want to dazzle them, not at first anyway—I never lost, that was only partially true: I never lost *unwillingly*. Here I opted to throw the first two games with a High Hand and a Straight, coming up short against the wolf's Four of a Kind and Flush. Good cards, but not dazzling. I kept my diamonds and jacks down, reading in the wolf's face that he was debauching himself grossly by an over-reliance on his kings and queens. He smiled at me, and I smiled back at him; he flashed his teeth, and I didn't back down.

A crowd was now gathering to watch, pointing their muzzles over one another's shoulders and looking curious as to what was about to unfold. An audience wasn't something I liked having since it meant I'd get a reputation that'd make hustling harder in these parts. Benny was nearby, watching nervously and biting the back of his paw white, black, and bloody. A bark from the wolf brought me back into reality, which I answered with a quick grin. I was greedy and this was perfect—I cut my eyes quick to look over and saw Carlos was still keeping his head bent over the drinks. Behind his back and above him were the four large amber blocks, embedded into the wall above the bar. Someone had said he kept his special stock of liquor up in there, saying it was because it helped keep the brew fresh. Among the stories that came out about the Electric Sewer, Carlos prided himself on his premium stock. The paintings hid the stocks, and it always seemed like a weird thing to do, but what I can say? Carlos was weird so what's weird to me might be about as normal as pie to a guy like him.

The rat was facing my direction, had looked up now and then to see where all the action was being diverted. I saw him glance up and motion to Elric, and Carlos had whispered something in the bull's ear, with Elric's horns bobbing up and down in understanding. The rat then headed away from the bar and disappeared behind a door, probably to attend to his own poker game.

Perfect.

"You ought to know when it's your time to go, twink," the wolf growled, sucking on an unlit cigar as he fingered his cards. It made me bristle, since I knew just his type—bitches like him only stuck it between their mouths for the taste, not to light the thing up. "Tell you what, I'll let you know you can have ten just for keeping me amused. And with them big lips of yours I bet you suck a golfball through a garden hose."

"So, is that your bet?" I asked. "Loser gets their dick wet by the other's lips?"

The wolf smiled, then muttered, "Be careful what you lay down there. Your mouth's writing a check your tail prolly can't cash."

"I bet that just gets you excited," I said casually.

"Actually, I've been jacking off the whole time," the wolf sneered. He leaned forward, and I heard three thumps come from underneath the table.

"Sounds like someone's not been getting any," I replied.

"I've just been waiting on someone like you to come along and get me off," came the wolf's answer. "You like them cards in your paws?"

"They're alright."

"I've been rubbing my dick on them. You see that glistening edge? That's my pre."

I leaned in and sniffed the rim of each card. I smirked.

"Smells like you got one helluva poor diet there. You ought to lay off the tuna and try some salmon, you'll be less impotent."

This made the others at the table laugh wildly. The wolf's eyes narrowed and flashed red.

"You think you're so hot, motherfucker?" he said.

"I'm burning up thinking of the ways you're gonna lose," I said back. "Or does the idea of being my bitch make you hard?"

"I've been hard and ready, just waiting to fuck your skull hard and fast."

I gave him another toothy grin. "You talk way too much for my liking, so much that you keep being a shitty deal."

"What's that mean?"

"Are you gonna bark all day little doggy, or are you gonna bite?" I replied. The quip cut the wolf but didn't throw him off the way I'd hoped. "Here, I'll make it easy for you: why don't you let me deal since you ain't doing the damn thing the right way?" The wolf looked to the others for a second, casting wary glances before he slid the deck my way.

Now here, I'll pause and say that up til now, yeah I was playing a little more honestly than I normally do. The main reason I never lose isn't because I've got some supernatural, Gladstone Gander kind of power to be lucky; it's because I know what I'm doing. Once that deck gets into my paws, I get straight into the mechanics: I know everyone's eyes aren't on me but on those cards, but I also know these are fellow canines–if they were felines, they'd have caught what I was doing as I shuffled the cards. It had the look of being random, but in actuality I was quickly looking and marking which card was gonna be an Ace, King, or Queen and marking the rest a different way to ensure my opponent would get a goose egg while I dealt myself the monsters.

How did I do this? I shifted each of the good cards to the bottom and dealt the rest as fast as possible, which were on the top while the bottoms were all mine.

I smirked inwardly at the cards I had while on the out I furrowed my brow as deep as I could, feigning a pissy attitude while I laid my cards down on the table. "Damn it all to shit and hellfire."

"So, folding already?" the wolf said. "Better get some mints and get them lips ready, motherfucker."

"Not yet," says me and itched the side of my muzzle. "Why don't we make this interesting?"

"What you got?"

"This," and I slid all the money Benny and I had to our names to the middle. "The whole damn pot. Pass or call it, doggy, your choice."

The wolf ran a tongue across his teeth, and I read him like a book. He wanted to bet conservatively and was folding his ears close to his head. I'd called that bluff as he pushed his winnings to the middle of the table, and his nostrils flared wide when he breathed, that deep chest betraying more than he'd intended. That's when I knew I had him and had something for his ass.

An Ace, an Eight, and three Twos.

"Three of a kind, fuckface," I announced. "Guess I win, but tell you what? I'll throw you ten, and you can suck my dick for being a good sport."

The wolf growled deep and stood up shouting, "You're a damn dirty cheat, you son of a whore!" He almost leaped across the table and grabbed the deck, flipping the bottom over and revealing the remaining Ace that I had there.

"That don't prove a thing," I said.

"You cheating bastard!"

"Now ain't that an ugly thing to say?" I smirked in my best Southern drawl, leaning back in my chair like I was Doc Holliday. "I guess this means I won't be getting my dick sucked after all."

There was the ruffle of movement, as a paw dove under his jacket and introduced a pistol to the conversation. Someone briefly gasped—I figured it was Benny—and a couple of the others at the table ducked for cover. Here, I kind of admit I was kind of nervous, if it weren't for that trust in the odds working in my favor: before the wolf could squeeze the trigger and pop off, I saw a looming black shadow out the corner of my eye dart past me, followed by the faint glimmer of an ivory horn sinking into soft flesh and punctuated by the sound of a squelching gurgle, like a melon being pulped, and the clattering of metal onto the floor.

I must've blinked, because it all happened in an instant. Elric was standing there over me, his horns impaled in the wolf's throat from behind. There was the wolf, struggling to talk as blood poured from his mouth and over the ivory horns, his paws gripping confused at the bull's points. Elric raised his head, ripping up and through the wolf's skull. Blood and teeth went flying, and a warm jet of liquid splashed up into my face, and the wolf crumpled back into his seat, his snout dangling by a single thread of skin and fur as his tongue flopped around like a fish on land for a second inside the gaping maw of what had been a head and a mouth before it went cold.

Elric stood over the corpse like a puppy after playing catch with their Pops. I caught a glimpse of Elric's cock in a not-so-faint outline pressed up against his pressed pants, and this made me think about what Benny had said about Fuqua as the bull ran a hoof along the edges of his hardness and breathed in deep lust, unzipping his length and beginning to stroke himself off as he watched the wolf's blood pour into a pool onto the floor. No one screamed, and no one was grossed out. This was just some of the things that were normal about the Electric Sewer.

When he was all done—following a trembling orgasm which he shot on the wolf's corpse—Elric turned to me and calmly said, "You. What's your name?"

"Tommy DeCarlo, what's it to you?" I said, trying to play

cool.

And just as cool, Elric answered, "You and your frail, come with me. Carlos wants you two."

The next thing that hit me that first time coming down the hallway was the smell. The further we got from the smell of either cheap liquor or high-end absinthe if you were really rich and bougie was the scent of old semen. I'd heard about that from someone else who had gotten this far, as there were bodies of mice, dogs, cats, and other cretins hopped up on pills or drunk off of orgasming so much that they could barely stand. Carlos loved to make his games interesting depending on who all wanted to play: if you wanted to dig in and try your paws at pinball, loser had to suck the winner's dick like they're a vacuum. Inside was another room that I peered in, where I had heard would wait Elric. If you lost the game he played, your ass better be as wide open as the Anton Anderson tunnel.

As I felt Benny's paw squeeze mine—which I let slip loose, ignoring his pleas—I sized Elric up. He's one of those guys whose face tells the story of his life. Red gashes marked his snout, his jowls, and one lid was almost closed over an eye. How he got that was a mystery that no one, at least the ones who talk about these things, ever talked about.

"Listen, if you're gonna kill me, can you make it quick?" I said, trying to make small talk. Here I was still kind of scared. I knew why I was making this walk, but you just didn't want to trust a guy who made folks into his sock puppets for fun.

"Who said anything about killing ya?" Elric answered back without looking at me.

"Then why are we back here?"

"Ya played good, boss was enjoying himself. Ya an ace at cards?"

"I'm decent," I replied, and thumbed my lucky deck in my

paws while the fur twitched between my shoulders violently. "So, this where the real action is?"

"Do ya really wanna know?"

"Never hurts to ask, especially when it helps my odds in the game."

"Tommy, don't push him," whispered Benny. "You're gonna get us eaten alive."

"I'm a tough chew," I spat.

I couldn't see his face, but I somehow knew Elric had heard and was grinning wide, having snorted. "Yer a mouthy kind of fucker, aren't ya?"

"It's gotten me this far."

"Mr. Carlos loves him some games too," Elric said. "He's always lookin' for the best paws to play against."

"So I've heard." I nodded, trying to keep cool.

"He also don't like to lose," added Elric.

"I've heard that too."

"But he also don't like to win without a challenge."

I nodded at this and said with all the flippancy I possessed, "Somebody's gonna win." What I added under my breath was the fact that that someone was gonna be me.

We stopped at a door that I'd get burned into my brain like a pain junkie looking to be branded by their domme. It wasn't ornate, and it wasn't even marked. It was just a door, plain and simple and wooden and drab as all can be. Elric rapped it five times. Shave and a haircut, that was the signal as I heard a latch on the other end come undone and the bolt sliding away and let me tell you I was smacked right in my face by all scents. Perfumes and jizz, old and fresh, wafted up when we walked in. Crouched on all fours in each corner were gimps, their heads covered with latex masks and their muzzles zipped up. Well, some of them—a couple were unzipped, and their maws were sucking off their handlers, whose eyes were closed in ecstasy and ignoring me and Elric for the most part.

The middle table sat Carlos, lording over it all, paws folded over one another as he eyed me coming inside. There were others seated on opposite ends of the square table, ears perked and muzzles lifted to get my scent. One of them, a Lab, growled until Carlos eased his nerves. Elric nodded quickly to Carlos then shuffled back into the shadows. "Tommy, right?" the rat asked.

"You know me?" I said. I'd never spoken two words to Carlos that didn't involve the order of a drink.

"Rum and coke, a Scotch on Fridays. Sometimes you get your frail to get you drinks off others."

"Sure thing."

"No tips, either."

That sent chills down my spine as I heard Benny whimper. I didn't buy a lot of the stories said about Carlos, but I still didn't pretend they were all false. Carlos never showed mercy to anyone; I don't think he even knew the meaning of the word. You forget to pay your tab, forget it, you were done for. Carlos didn't forgive; he didn't forget.

"What brings you here?" Carlos queried.

"I'm here to make some real money."

This earned a laugh from the guys at the table.

Everyone except Carlos. He was eyeing me, watching my eyes and my face. Benny didn't factor into anything; I was the one playing.

"I'm pretty clean," I said and held up Benny's purse. "And I'm good for it too."

"Is that so," Carlos said.

It wasn't a question, but I answered it all the same. "Yeah, it is so. What of it, old man?"

I guess I shouldn't have been nearly as glib as I was. I could feel the tension bristle in the air, as my own fur stood on end from all the static. But Carlos was only smiling, leaning back in his chair as the jelly rolls of his large stomach reclined with him.

"Elric," Carlos began, "Two-Four-Eight-Zero-One, please?" I heard the bull snort a response and felt his presence disappear for a second. Carlos smiled when Elric returned. He had a gimp trembling in his hooves as Carlos nodded. "We don't like cheaters," Carlos said to me and Benny with a smile, gesturing to the gimp.

Elric grinned wide and the wide-flaring nostrils seemed to exude fire. The gimp seemed to forget their place as blind panic surged through their body, struggling and heaving, but even I could've told him it was no use, especially when in one quick and foul motion those hooves of Elric's crushed the gimp's left arm bones into dust leaving it dangling limp and useless like a rubber glove. Then he moved onto the second and then it was the gimp who crumpled to the ground.

From beneath their mask, Benny and I heard the screams. Benny wobbled on his feet and gripped my forelimb tight to steady himself, but I muttered forcefully, "For crike's sakes get ahold of yourself!"

"He okay?" Carlos asks, gesturing to the dalmatian.

"Nothing that a little whiskey can't fix."

"Savio."

The calico pawed over his glass to Benny, and he clutched it with both paws trembling as we saw Elric continue his playtime. The gimp was trying to back away now with their legs, the only functional things that they had going for them when Elric flipped them over like a pancake onto their stomach, back and tail facing the bull as Elric reached into his pants and pulled out a knife. He lifted the blade high over his horns and then brought it down, hard, into the gimp, and me and Benny heard that half-muted scream fill the entire backroom.

I thought it was all over then, but something must've gone wrong or Elric's aim wasn't too good as the knife came out of the gimp, pulling a mist of blood behind it, and then came back down again and again. With the final jab, Elric sheared down the length of the gimp's back, ripping through muscle and bone and fur and skin and latex as the gimp coughed out their death screams. But death wasn't coming, not yet, anyway, as Elric bent over him and grabbed the gimp's back, opening him wide thanks to the incision that he made and exposing his ribs and spinal column for all of us, the red ooze dripping heavily to the floor as someone vomited and others choked theirs back.

Elric wasn't through with the gimp: the bull undid his pants and let his raging black cock out, precum dribbling the ground as he began to fuck the gimp's exposed anatomy. Blood and bile from a futilely pumping liver and kidney got into the faces of everyone who was nearby, and the smell of someone else puking hit my senses as I heard one of the dommes nearby commanding their gimp to clean it up.

"Holy fuck," I breathed.

Carlos pointed out. "Elric's been eyeing that one for a month. Good chance to let him show off."

"You won't have to worry about me," I said to Carlos, as I saw the bull spray his jizz on the gimp's now-stilled heart. "So, can I play?"

The other players around Carlos' table looked to the rat, as he himself leaned back and set his jaw and scratched the side of his nose. Finally, he said to the calico next to him, "Savio, make room."

The calico scooted over, and I grabbed a chair, Benny behind me with a nervous paw on my shoulder. Carlos slid the deck my way, but I said, "Thanks, but I got my own if that's all right." Once more the other players looked to Carlos, who shrugged and waved an approving gesture. I saw Benny shake his head side to side, knowing what was coming next from me, but I ignored him , whipping my deck and starting first with the Sybil Cut, an elegant bit of showmanship any mook can do with two paws.

I followed this up with the Riffle Shuffle, randomizing the cards thoroughly so no one could say since it was my deck I was about to cheat. I then moved into the one-pawed shuffle, cutting the deck into two and ended with a Cascade, the cards flowing into the palm of my paw like water as I spread and dealt the cards out to each player.

"This boy's good," smirked the calico named Savio as he picked up his cards.

Now, here I'll tell you that the game can either take minutes or any hour. You wanna get it down to the minutes section because if you're good, you can easily bluff your way into having your opponent submit. Anything longer than that is just showing off.

"I'm out," said Savio.

"Damn, me too," said another, a fellow beagle, which was quickly followed by two more around the table, until it was getting to be just me and Carlos.

The rat sipped on his drink and raked the edges of his cards with a claw. His eyes never met mine, making it hard to read him.

"I'm in," Carlos muttered, raising his pot by forty with the whole stake now up by five hundred. He then raised his eyes to mine. "You, boy?"

Benny kept his eyes close to my deck, trying not to betray my cards. My tail gave a little wag even as I was stoic as a judge.

"I'm gonna raise you a hundred," I said.

"Helluva pot," Carlos muttered. "Must be feeling pretty good or pretty dumb right now."

I laughed. "Dumb would be if we walked out of here without a story to tell folks on the outside."

Carlos grinned. "I'll raise five hundred." Benny inhaled behind my ear, just as I felt his claws dig into my shoulder. "Something wrong with your friend?"

"Nothing that a little wager won't fix," I said, shrugging Benny off. "Check Ace, high five-forty."

"This is a man's game, kid. Make it worthwhile."

Thinking on this, I glanced at my cards and then back at Carlos and chuckled. "You know, I'm thinking you're right. Better than worthwhile, how about interesting?"

"I'm listening," Carlos answered, his tiny ears wriggling.

"Loser kisses the other's tip," I said. "Make their humiliation more perfect."

"You know what you want," Carlos said. "You have a flair for virility. That talent could feed many who harness it."

"So I've heard," I grinned, then winked at Benny. "Wanna have a taste of it, old man?"

Again came that winking leer as Carlos replied, "In due time. Could always be more than just kissing my dick. Ain't that right, Savio?" I looked up and saw the calico grin. I saw a well-hung beast who had no modesty about what he had. Too bad I was about to disappoint him and Carlos.

"Oh go ahead, try me," I said. "I'm ready for your worst."

"Tommy, don't..." Benny warned, but I shushed him, my tone sharp. He was breaking my concentration.

"Won't like my worst, boy," Carlos said behind a half-smile. "Could just flatten you on your tail right here and now. Let Elric show you boys the way out for losers and we can call it a night."

"Or I can step up to you like a real man," I said, "and show you what I got for that ass."

Carlos laughed. "I'll raise you a good, hour-long blowjob."

I smiled. "Not just the tip, huh?"

"Can't take the heat?"

"These stakes are getting interesting. How about I see that and raise you a pounding right here in front of your clients? None of that kinky, knife-to-the-back gay shit either."

Carlos only chuckled. "Be careful, boy."

"How's this?" I growled and slid the whole purse to the middle. "Twenty-five hundred and some change right there. And Benny's ass over here is yours for the taking." I heard Benny whisper my name frantically, but I ignored him. "How about it, old man? You ready to fold yet?"

"Always this fast?" Carlos asked behind a chuckle.

"My speed is the stuff of nightmares. Your move, old man."

"You don't know what you're up against, kid," Savio said into my other ear, at the same time nibbling along the edge, running his paws along my thighs. My tail stiffened when I felt him squeeze my cock and give a hard jerk. Benny growled, and he backed off for a second. "Walk away now and save yourself the trouble."

"What's the matter, rat?" I said, ignoring the warning. "Afraid that a boy like me is about to come after your ass?"

Carlos said. "Full of surprises, huh?"

"Only one way to find out. So what do you say, rat?" I asked.

Carlos winked. "I say you don't want to know what I bet next. I fold."

I grinned and laid my cards on the table. "Full house. Suck on that, old man."

Carlos sighed. Laying his deck slowly, card by card, on the table like he did was like a nail being drilled into my coffin.

A straight flush.

All the cards were the same suit.

My maw hung open, and my heart was close to jumping out of my chest. Savio and the rest of the players around Carlos' table were grinning, as Benny gripped my shoulder so tight that I felt blood draw and clot up against my fur.

Carlos had won.

And I had lost all of my money.

"Well now," Carlos began, looking inside the purse. "Let's talk."

I was silent. What could I say? I'd lost—for the first time in my life I had lost in a game I thought I had perfected.

"About a grand short of what you bet, boy," the rat continued. "I usually let Elric beat the shit out of little snots like you or break your paws when payment's not forthcoming. But there's more entertaining ways to get what's owed to me. For now," Carlos said and snapped out to Elric, and the bull was like a 12 o'clock shadow swooping over Benny and me, "this is the end of your game."

The room was plain but strangely clean, something I wasn't expecting at all. Tile floors and wood paneling from probably before I was born. A single window pulled shut and caked with a lot of grime and dust as lights flickered in from the outside and shined across my chest. I was on the edge of a bed, naked, my clothes in a heap near the hamper underneath a window. There was a door, bolted from the outside; the only way out was to do what I had to do and then I could leave, and that was all dependent on if the debts were satisfied.

All that bluster I was saying, how no one was unbeatable.

And here was my ass about to get it because I was beaten.

Both paws were cuffed to the bedframe. Nothing special

about this either, just a typical lock wrapped tight around my left wrist while its brother was connected by a link as thick as my thumb across the right and both rattled like castanets on the metal post, where a sharp and jagged edge slid up against my ulnar bone. On both sides next to me were twin little tables. One had a glass of water resting with more peace than I was gonna get, and on the other was a half-broken lamp with a burnt out lightbulb. The drawer of this one was pulled halfway out, and I could see the glint of something metallic winking at me thanks to the dim lighting which came in from the single old light bulb above my head.

I was stripped naked, my clothes torn off me by Elric and the surface smooth and shiny from where my fur had been shaved off. Carlos said it was because his clients liked bare chests and Elric wasn't gentle when he did it. The smell of shaving cream was in the air, and it made me sicker but, and call it a mix of fear and excitement, my brown nipples were standing on end as I glared at the door, waiting on whatever was about to happen to happen.

Carlos had said he enjoyed playing me. The game had been good, Carlos had had a good time, but I'd lost, and debts had to be paid.

"Ordinarily," Carlos had said, watching off to the side as Elric took his straight razor and cut none too gently across my chest, "I'd have Elric use you for fun. Hell, looks like he's already got a woody. But this will be more enjoyable for a client who owes me too and will square us away."

I listened to every sound on the outside of that door. Every creak, every cough, even the damn wind blowing through the upstairs. Upstairs in the Electric Sewer was a place no one really ever saw unless it was a special occasion or you paid for it.

And brother, was I paying for it.

But I sat there listening and I was thinking: once this was all over, I was gonna come back, back here, and back to that table. It was gonna be worth it, even if I had to endure this first.

I listened to the key in the grill shoot home and the latch slide back, followed by a jiggle of the door handle. The door itself swung inward, and I caught the scent of who's coming in, along with the smell of something awful.

Feline, mixed with gods know what kind of tobacco smoke.

Only a feline would have that kind of disregard for the senses of a canine.

"Bet you thought I'd be Elric, didn't you?" said Savio, filling the whole of the doorway. "Cuffs are usually his M.O., but I like that kinky gay shit too."

When he was sitting down during Carlos' game, I hadn't had any idea how huge he was, with massive broad shoulders on a frame which blocked out the whole of the outside. Not as huge as Elric, but bigger than I thought. His shirt was already off, showcasing the white-orange-black pattering all over his furred self, and his pants were partly undone, down to the boxers. Both ears were pierced with twin bobby pins.

"You're not my type," I quipped, just as Savio took a long drag on his cigarette and blew it in my face. The haze hit me like a sledgehammer, and red alarms blared up and down inside my sinus cavities.

"Don't matter what your type is," replied Savio, closing the door behind him. He came closer, dabbing some ashes off to the side. "You were out of your league coming here tonight. You couldn't pay up so your ass belongs to me."

"Is this your debt to Carlos?" I asked. Savio nodded and then pulled out one of those cheap disposable cameras you can get from any pharmacy counter from his pants pocket.

"I got it easier than the other fucks," Savio explained. "All I owe Carlos is a few pictures for his personal amusement."

I ground my teeth at that, but it was no one's fault except mine. I needed to be stronger and faster and bolder. I needed to be a lot of fucking things, and I couldn't get to them because I'd fucked this up so bad.

I needed above all else to get out of here and show these Electric Sewer bitches who was the boss.

I wanted to ask where Benny was, but before the words left my maw Savio was on me, knees pinning my arms to the bed or rather he'd put his right paw over my snout. The cigarette was dangling between the digits of his left, its orange ember dancing down my neck until he buried it along the side of my chest.

I wanted to scream.

Did scream, right into the meat of his paw.

It was a muffled song of pain. If anyone heard, no one would've cared.

That was just how it was in the Electric Sewer.

"Looks like someone liked that," Savio smirked as he took his paw away from my snout. I sucked in gusts of air like I couldn't get enough of it, but the pain seared into me like the cigarette was still being jabbed into me.

And then Savio did it again. And again, and again.

Seven times in total, until the cigarette was all done and so was he, but not before he muttered, "Almost forgot," and snapped away on his camera. "Carlos would kill me if I didn't get those. He cums real hard when he sees this kinda stuff."

Fighting back tears was impossible as I bucked and thrashed. Savio looked down at me with little sympathy, or any emotion on his face. His whiskers were like thin lines against the dim light, and the silhouette of his ears resembled bull horns and made me wonder, in the black hole of pain I was in in the back of my mind, if this was really Elric instead.

When he stopped, I noticed that he'd glided out of his pants and was fully erect. Another flash of light from the outside showed off the veins of that kitty's cock pulsating like a firehose furiously pumping water to put out a raging fire. I made the feeblest attempt at jerking my wrist free before I felt the first pinch of the metal scrape away my fur and dig into the skin beneath, and I felt the blood trickle down and up into my armpit.

"I don't like all that screaming," Savio explained and gripped my throat hard and forced my mouth open. "Bite me and I don't care what Carlos says, but I'll kill you if you bite me. You got it?"

I nodded that I understood as he put himself past my paw and I felt the tip of his dick touch the back of my throat. I coughed and gagged, some saliva and drool oozed up underneath his foreskin and pooled into his center.

"Suck me off, bitch," the feline moaned, grabbing the back of my head and thrusting full-force in and out of my mouth. I held my jaws wide and prayed that my teeth didn't scrape up against him, then closed my lips around his full length. Suddenly I was caught by surprise as Savio brushed a paw against my nose, petting and savoring this moment, then leaned close and nuzzled into my neck, inhaling my scent. That subtle shift caught me off-guard, and I was suddenly finding myself aroused at the sensation, his long and rough tongue rolling up underneath my folds as he put the stress on my cuffed wrist to pull me closer to him.

I was able to glean his own scent: sensitive and fine on the one paw like all felines, then strong and dominating on the other. I was being let into a private space of intimacy which was about to exist between just the two of us, regardless of the circumstances happening as his touching and petting made me shiver and wag, his paws quick and sure about where they exploring. Suddenly I felt a great force part my ass cheeks and penetrate my hole–not his dick, not yet, but first one digit and then two, followed by three with them all fitting in and forcing the hole wider.

I gasped and winced on cue, as the slickness of his digits made the sensation rough but pleasant, and I panted hard and heavy. The little hole was widening, as Savio spread my legs open and stretched me out, pausing a couple times to let me enjoy the fullness, and I could not resist my gag reflex about to kick in as the saliva ran into my nose. It didn't matter if it all was hurting. I was squeezing the pain out, squeezing my eyes shut while he fucked my face over and over.

He paused when he heard me give off a gagging cough. "Did that hurt?" he asked solemnly. "Good. Gotta say, if this whole cardsharp thing don't work out, you could be someone's fuck-toy. They can call you Golden Throat because damn you almost made me bust one there."

"Are we done?" I gasped out.

Savio shook his head. "Not yet. Spread 'em."

I resisted.

"Are you gonna spread 'em for me, or do I have to do it?"

"You're not gonna fit," I said. "You felt it, I'm too tight for you to enjoy yourself."

Savio smirked and flashed me a wink. "You say that like it's impossible. There's always a way if you know how."

I gulped, not quite knowing what it was he planned to do. Savio hooked his paws around my hips and held my legs back, almost up to my head and exposing my backside to him. "Such a slutty ass," he said grinning as he spat into my gaping hole as glistening pre from his hungry dick fell onto the bed. Click and snap went the camera, and my ears burned hot, furthered when

I felt his digits again explore my hole, twisting and spreading and widening and I waited until he found some satisfaction at its size. There was none—he hissed momentarily in frustration and then I saw a paw dip towards the table and into the open drawer. That's when I saw what it was that was gleaming and catching the night's light.

A pair of scissors.

The blades were waxed and bound, and as if for dramatic gesture Savio snapped them open and closed a couple times, showing off that they were in fact functional. I offered no resistance as the wetness at my own tip dripped down into my navel. I was shivering and excited and somehow scared all at once from what was about to happen next. Savio wasn't nice when he threw the scissors into me; that first thrust felt like it had stabbed me in my soul. I felt it in my chest, each stabbing pain from every seesaw prod he made. Up and down, up and down, trying to get me wider, his other paw snapping away on the camera as I felt my blood gush down my ass crack and dry in sticky clumps along my tail and cling to the bed.

"What'd I say about all that screamin'?" Savio spat. Before I could answer, another yipping scream escaped from my jaws as Savio began opening the scissors, laughing as he did so and opening and shutting them in the same way as he'd shown me before. "Hmm, you're certainly looking wide enough now," he says, "but I think you can learn to be a little more open."

"Why…why are you doing this?" I gasped.

Savio smiled and shrugged. "Carlos likes you way too fucking much. First time I ever lost to him I had to suck off that bastard Elric. Couldn't eat solid food for a month after that. You lose and only get to be my playdate. It's not fair, but hey," grinned Savio, "Carlos didn't say I had to leave you looking pretty when it's all done with. Like the pretty words you said earlier...which reminds me, that silver tongue of yours is something you don't need and it pissed me off hearing you talk."

At this, he pulled the scissors out of my ass and held my maw wide. The calico pulled my tongue out of my head and held the tip between the blades.

I shook my head, pleading.

Savio shook his, disagreeing as he opened the blades wide and then brought them down. The first sensation was like being hit by a bolt of lightning that I didn't have time to really register the second, or the third or the fifth, until finally I tasted warm, tangy, and sticky liquid pour down my throat and dribble down my chin.

Savio was laughing now, and in my glazed and dazed vision I saw he had something clutched between the digits of his left paw, which he tossed behind his back and landed with a wet thud against the wall.

"Now you're all mine for the taking," he said.

He was aiming his dick now at my ass, having smeared himself with plenty of spit and blood for lubrication. Savio placed his head at my entrance, then roughly drove himself up my ass until he was almost as embedded as Elric had been up in that gimp's body. I know I screamed out—had to have screamed, and I saw little black stars at the edge of my vision which soon faded as Savio started to thrust in and out of me. I felt the calico grab my ears and tightly in his free paw and shove my head down onto my cock, forcing me to suck myself off as deep as I could go and ignoring my distorted cries from his painful anal invasion.

"Fuck, you're still fucking tight!" laughed Savio, and he slowed himself down, but only just a little. I craved the relaxation, the shift in my spine and the position made me feel like everything inside me was cramping up. I realized that this may have been why I was as tight as I was around his dick, but I wasn't gonna tell him that.

When Savio entered me, I felt the rough-as-iron hardness of his cock, and I thought I was gonna be split in half, with the base of my asshole feeling like it was a pulsating button. Savio leaned in and grabbed my ruff in his muzzle right before he thrusted again and again into me, his knot tight and hard, and I know he's about to bust a nut sooner rather than later. My ass formed like a seal around his knot and my dick couldn't resist as I too was hard and spurting pre-cum all over myself, aroused at my own arousal.

I hadn't realized that Savio had overestimated his balance when he first slid into me and slipped a bit, collapsing flat onto my stomach and gasping and moaning as I felt his pressure release at the same time mine did and then felt the shear lightning of that metal cut hard into my right wrist. Blood poured down my arm as Savio filled me up, and I was aware of Savio twitching and moaning on top of me through the dim light of utter ecstasy. He then went stiff and still, and in seconds I listened to the mewling snores which came out of the calico.

Pain wracked every inch of my body. I knew that when the calico woke back up the wheel was gonna turn, and the cycle was about to start up again. I didn't want to think about what else could he possibly do. Break my digits, chop off my dick and fuck me with it?

Then a savage thought rent itself through my mind, as if everything around me was restarting, and the dirty rough sex was just a nightmare of bliss:

Lubrication.

Blood was a lubricant. Savio had made that shit clear.

Blood worked just as good as any cream. Someone could stab you then grease their dick up before fucking you if you were dry, all with your own blood. Until it clotted, blood was just as slick as oil.

I'd read in an old science mag they called this "degloving". Don't ask me what the technical term used in hospitals is, and it is just how it's described. Peeling off a glove from your paw or hoof so that it ends up inside-out. Same thing, just with fur and skin instead of latex and silk glove.

Real nasty, bloody, and yeah...not pleasant. And if I was about to do it, I knew it would hurt like a son of a whore. Cut too deep and I'll bleed out–but what choice did I have? Savio was gonna snap out of his stupor any moment now, and he'd either play with me more until he was satisfied I'd paid off my debt. Or kill me, depending on what him, Carlos, or Elric felt like. This was a lot like poker, running over the odds and thinking of each bluff and raised stake. And what if I did get out, then what? I still needed to slip out of the other cuff. As far as I could see, Savio didn't have a key on him and if he did, I was gonna have to search him til I found it.

I looked at the lefty and decided that I'll cross that bridge when I got to it. I took a hard and deep breath, and I listened to Savio moan something, thinking I was just exhaling my own pleasure after cumming. Wetting my lips and taking another hard breath and keying myself up as high as I could, and jammed my wrist into that jagged edge, almost passing out, not from the pain but because there was none, only this dull sense of pressure and faint heat. Blood dropped and rolled in fat globs down into the stained quill of the mattress and settled into a darker color once they'd pooled.

Then I curved my wrist around the jagged chunk, careful not to bear too much or else I'd sever the nerves and bleed out and lead the edge like it was an ancient scimitar doing its nasty, needed work on some poor bastard. I want to say I felt nothing at first, the sensations were dim and the warmth more like sunning myself on a warm summer's day. The metal popped through fur and skin and parted through the veins, the blood rolling down in a steady flow that I thought was almost like water from a faucet.

Slowly and carefully I twisted my wrist, splitting the tight skin and slick, matted fur. There was a weird tingling sensation all across the spectrum, and my paw jittered once before caving in on itself, the nerves deadening. I didn't think I'd be using that paw ever again, a realization made possible by all the heat-gore coming down fast. The skin and fur was moving, like taking off a bracelet but that'd be dumb–it was more like taking off a glove. But I was close, seeing that I was at the halfway point, at about the back of my wrist now and kept at it.

I could see the tendons exposed in its wet strands as the fur wrinkled and bunched up with every pull and tug. I revolved, twisted, and turned, screaming away the pain that raged, sunk and twisted my paw as Savio squirmed and life slowly started coming back to him.

Time was running out.

Panic surged with all the fury of electricity running across the sky, and I drove the metal edge as deeply into the back of my paw as I could, damning whatever pain, whatever heat, whatever whatever I felt as I yanked my paw back towards me. This brought a fine and juicy torrent of spatter into my face and coated my nose, misted my eyes, and filled my mouth.

But the job was done, the cuff which had kept my right wrist prisoner clattering empty against the bed post. I spared a quick glance at the results of my operation: the digits were a thick streak of red, the whole paw resembling slick and sticky latex glove, as if someone had slathered that whole fucking arm with the stuff. I could see tendons glistening in that dim light and the musculature looked just like spaghetti sauce.

I laid there for what felt like forever looking at it, even though the whole thing was just a few bite-sized seconds, and thought hard about my next move. It came to me when Savio raised his head and through dilated eyes he could see that something was up before the copper scent of all that blood caused his nostrils to flare with each deep breath. His back arched, and he looked my way and, I don't know how, but I managed to grip my stump of a paw around that glass of water and smash it into his face.

Savio shot up and flew from the bed, hissing and growling as he clawed at his face to pick out the glass, thrashing wildly from the wall to the floor and back again with his tail whipping around like a beheaded snake. I got a sick pleasure from watching him scream, but then a brief wave of concern washed over me when I saw him edge closer to the window. I made a feeble move to warn him, but it was too late: almost like a Tex Avery cartoon, the window wrapped itself around Savio and then broke into a million little shards as the calico fell right through and out the other side, with the sickening thud of death coming next followed by someone on the sidewalk screaming.

I pushed aside any curiosity I'd have had while I looked around the room. I saw his pants, the belt still attached to its loops, and almost broke my hip stretching out to hook my foot around it to bring up to my paws, first maneuvering it to my mouth and then to my left paw, where I took the belt out and used the sharp prong to pick the lock and free myself.

Before I left that room, I found the camera lying on the floor beside the bed. With a toss that would've made Tomcat Seaver proud, I pitched that fucker out the window and listened for a second to the crash as it collapsed against the ground next to its owner.

Outside in the hall, seemed like everyone had left what they were doing to check out what was happening. I still had to be careful, ditching the main stairway to find a barely used emergency exit and made my exit.

I probably walked five miles that night, keeping my mangled paw clutched tight against my chest and spitting blood every time my mouth filled up with it. I couldn't go back to mine and Benny's place—the landlord had already probably locked us out since we hadn't paid any of the rent.

Benny...

My fur twitched violently, and my stomach cramped.

I had no money to my name. Nowhere to go, no one to go to. Even if I had wanted to attempt a rescue of Benny, I knew it was a suicide mission. And then I had to ask myself if I even still cared. If I hadn't listened to Benny, none of this would've happened and I'd be getting my rocks off instead of getting rocked. Benny was the root of all this, and if I kept thinking about him instead of myself I was gonna get in deeper shit than I already was in.

But, even with that logic ahead of me, I couldn't quite bring myself to say "fuck 'em". I owed Benny, and while I couldn't dwell on whatever situation he was in right now, I didn't let it fall too far from my mind.

I broke into a pharmacy on 59th and Elm, using the elbow of my left arm, and did all the first aid stuff I could think of. I screamed and growled reflexively after dunking my mangled paw into the sink full of alcohol, the dozen or so bottles clattering aimlessly on the floor around while I thrashed from the burning pain. I probably went through seven rolls of bandages, each one soaked before the blood stopped and the gauze took hold.

Good enough, just 'til I managed to figure out my next move. Walk around anywhere around the Electric Sewer and you're bound to find the right thing you need at the moment you need it most. And for me, that just ended up becoming an empty alleyway which I bunked in, passing out for several hours until I was woken up by a cop who busted me for being drunk.

Like I said, walk around anywhere around the Electric Sewer and you're bound to find the right thing you need at the moment you need it most and at that moment I knew they don't let folks die in jail, so the jailhouse infirmary took care of my paw and bandaged up my cigarette burns. The docs told me it takes about a month, maybe two, for it all to heal properly. I told them I didn't have a month, forming the words the best I could. Not when revenge burns hotter than hellfire coal inside my chest.

In the end, they insisted, especially when one of the nurses revealed that I'd said under the influence of ether that I had nowhere to go and no one to go to. Plus, I needed to learn how to reuse that paw after damaging the nerves like I had.

It was true, I didn't have anything except wanting to get out and get back in the game. But I knew I needed rest and I needed to get my head right. Go in there hot-headed and hot-tailed and I'd fuck up yet again and be someone else's fuck toy.

So in the three months I took in rehab at the hospital, I did my best not to think about my paw, the docs, or even jail. I thought about how I had got cocky, how I got Benny and I in a bad situation because I wasn't thinking and didn't make the right moves.

But I didn't even need to think about Benny either.

Not right now.

All I needed to think about was winning.

That and making sure that the doctors or nurses didn't see

me slipping the scalpel into my pants pocket while they worked on me.

At the end of those months I was let out, and I still couldn't jump into things like I wanted to. I just needed to wait. I just needed to sit still and think.

I just needed something to give me that one lucky in.

And it just so happened that I was in a bar across from the Electric Sewer when I got one.

It was just a regular dive, with no atmosphere, full of the haze of cigarette smoke and the boozy lifeless jazz coming out from a half-dead jukebox. Whatever crowd there was just wanted to drink and pretend to forget about everything for a couple hours; there's no snatches of conversation, no mirth, hell I'll just say it—place was a dump and a half, but it was the only place I felt I could get a drink of something. Water in a grimy glass, since it was the only thing I could afford, trying to ignore the pain throbbing in my paw when the bartender, a fennec, looked down her slim and slender nose at me, and her sharp ears twitched.

"What?" I asked, slightly nettled and ready to fight if I had to.

"You look familiar," she said, paws digging into a glass and cleaning abysmally. "You ever been around here?"

"Nope."

She shrugged and turned her back on me for a few moments, and I thought that was the end of that when she glanced round my way once again, leaning forward with one paw on her hip and resting her forelimb on the bar. "Listen kid, I know times is tough all around, but a pretty boy like you don't need to be drinking alone you know."

"Sounds like good advice."

"It's about as free as that water you're putting a lickin' on.

You got someone you can go home to?"

"You always this chatty with patrons?"

"Just the ones who interest me," she replied, noticing my paw for the first time. "You look like you had one helluva tough break there. Does it hurt?"

"Comes and goes. What's with the third degree?"

Her ears blushed, and she looked down. "You don't stink like most dogs around here."

I scoffed. "Thanks."

"No, I mean it. You don't look like you just came in from hell. You look like you've got a reason to give a damn about something."

"You can tell all that just by looking at me?" I quipped.

"Hon, it's my specialty. It's what I do, and what I can tell you is that that tough break you got didn't break you: you got the swag of a kid just waiting for one lucky break to come their way."

"That's pretty ubiquitous. Well, I can tell you I just got out of the hospital so that's why I'm clean."

"Cause of your paw?"

I nodded. "And now I'm just trying to figure out where I'm gonna go from here."

"And have you?"

"Well, I ain't gonna find it at the bottom of this glass, that's for sure."

The waitress clicked her teeth together, her batwing-like ears folding flat to her skull. "Well, hon, I can tell you that things do look kinda grim for you now, but you probably should feel better getting it off your chest talking to me instead of bottling it up."

I disagreed, but I said, "Thanks for listening. You really must do that to all your customers."

"Just the sad sacks," she said.

"Thanks."

"And you kind of remind me of an ex of mine from a long time ago."

"Did you love him?" I asked, folding behind a smirk.

"He was a bastard," she said. "But he had a big dick and knew how to use it." She was looking down into my lap at the bulge that was growing, and I was looking up at her and down her shirt where I was seeing her perky C-cups jiggling out from their bust, and my tail swished from side to side.

"Look," she says, "I can walk away from the bar for about ten minutes before the winos think it's a free-for-all."

"I'm not a whore," I say.

The fennec sighs. "I know, I'm sorry. I don't know what I was..."

"But I can be your whore," I finished. "Thousand bucks, and I can be your big-dick ex all you want."

I waited to see if she would be desperate enough to accept that offer. She said nothing and then crossed the length of the bar to the divider, opening it and beckoning me behind. She then grabbed me by my shirt collar and pulled me towards her back room.

"This is happening," she said. "Do you have a condom?"

"Sure," I answer, "in my pocket."

Eleven minutes later and I walk out of there a thousand dollars richer and with the smell of a freshly fucked fennec wafting off my fur. Before I crossed the street back to the Electric Sewer, I remember the condom still strapped on my dick. I reach inside my pants and pull it off, grinning at the torn bit of contraception. It wasn't my fault she didn't specify if the condom was unused, right?

Marching back inside the Electric Sewer, I felt everyone's

eyes on me. I cut my own glances to the bar, where I didn't expect Carlos to be stationed and cut a path to the hallway I'd walked down that first time, everyone parting out of my way like I'm Moses and they're the waves of the Red Sea when I suddenly felt a hard pressure in my chest.

I hadn't been looking. If I had, I'd have noticed the hoof and the strong-as-hell arm it was connected to.

"Whoa there, hotshot," Elric said, standing in my way.

"What's up?" I greeted him. "Fuck anyone raw lately?"

"Just where the fuck do ya think yer going?"

"Gonna see a man about a card game," I replied.

Elric took one hard and long glance at me and sighed something that I took to be an attempt at pity. "Look, kid, I don't wanna be the guy to break it all to ya...actually, hell with that, I love to be that guy. Ya gotta lotta nerve comin' back in here after last time."

"I just wanna play the game fair and square," I said, and met the bull's hard, cold eyes.

For a second I thought Elric was going to just kill me and have his way with my corpse in front of everyone. I braced my body for it. Instead, he shrugged and checked me over, making sure I had no guns or nothing. He was patting down my sides and stroking my tail, but he didn't check my ruff for the scalpel, which I'd taped down and covered up as good as possible, then he decided I was clean. Like before, he gestured me to the back. Like before, the smell of fresh cum hit my nose along with the moans and groans of those being played with and played.

And like before, when the door swung open, all the eyes in Carlos' card room turned to meet me. All the gimps were satisfying their masters, not acknowledging me one bit. Except for one, who was strapped to the wall and clad in latex, a ballgag stuffed into their maw. From the exposed areas at the ass, groin, and armpits I could see that they'd been shaved with a straight razor, and cruelly too–sores were broken out all over this gimp's body, but I could tell by their scent just who it was.

"Benny," I mouthed. Somehow he heard me and lifted his head, our eyes meeting as he offered a pitiful whimper my way. Looking down at his center, I noticed an odd device attached to his dick: it was a clear tube which covered the whole of his cock with the underside palpitating his balls, as a long hose extended from this and out the other side of the wall. It looked like a device for teats, breast feeding and all that, but apparently worked great for milking jism out of dicks. With a latex liner and aluminum constriction rings and nozzle over the top for lube, it'd feel like a pussy or an asshole or a mouth sucking you off good and right.

From here several tubes and lines went into the wall, as a plastic box containing the pump rested on the floor beside him, marked at maximum elongation and pulling his cock back and forth as the aluminum rings teased and ran over the edge of his head and keeping his shaft rock solid. Suddenly a loud yell escaped out of his muzzle, and he shot his load down the tube and it was immediately absorbed by the machine, turned completely white and sucked back up by the pump and into the wall.

Carlos and everyone else in the room just laughed as they watch Benny spray his natural juice as he breathed hard behind his ball gag, groaning and trembling as the orgasm quickly faded away and nothing but pain filled his whimpering cries. But it wasn't long before a second one built up behind that one, and he continued to fill the tubes with white, the pulsator clicking and pumping as Carlos guided its crazy sounds like a conductor with his paws, waving the remote control around pressing the button for more power. That's when I remembered the strange taste of the Electric Sewer's drink Carlos called "the Milk". You had to be a high-paying, high-rolling patron to afford it. So naturally I'd stolen a sip or three from someone who had.

But Benny had been right.

Carlos was into some fucked-up shit.

As another whimper left Benny's mouth after what was probably his eighth orgasm, my eyes did the talking for me: I knew I'd fucked up, but I was about to make it better.

He just had to trust me.

"Heard you were dead, kid," Carlos said, shifting in his seat as he shuffled a deck in his paws.

My deck.

"And I heard you were down a player," I snapped, walking towards the table.

"What can I say, the odds didn't favor either of us," the rat said. "Why you here?" He cuts his eyes towards Benny then back to me, curling the mini-whiskers along his snout. "Revenge?"

"Revenge? Yeah, I guess," I replied, and felt Elric put a hoof on my shoulder. I quickly added, "But nothing like that. I wanna play you, Carlos."

"Is that all?" He looked down at my paw, which I hid behind my back.

I shrugged. "Just let me into this game, Carlos, and if I lose you'll never see me again. Elric can beat me to death, cut my head off and fuck the stump. I'll be dead so I won't care. Or you can let me in and let me show you what I got."

"Admirable. But not every bastard becomes so obsessed with beating me."

"To be honest, you cast a spell over me."

Carlos chuckled. "Pretty words."

"Yeah well, thank fuck Savio didn't cut my tongue off all the way."

"Yeah, should've warned you about him. You owe me some pictures by the way. What are the terms if you win?"

I smirked. "Just winning."

"That's it?"

"That's it. You can keep the money, I just want to prove I have what it takes to be a better man than you."

The silence rang out in the card room like a bell, as Carlos shifted his weight in his chair, thinking. "I'm touched, kid. How's about this, if you win you get your frail back."

Benny lifted his head up and our eyes met up, new hope beginning to rise in his chest. I could save him and redeem my lost pride all in one go, if I literally played my cards right.

"Yeah?" I replied. "Just like that? I get him back if I win?"

"Yeah," Carlos says. "No tricks."

"Yeah?"

"Yeah. Cries too much anyway. Gives his jizz a weird aftertaste my customers haven't liked since we hooked him up months ago. You know, like Diet Coke and rum."

"I'm a Coke Zero guy, myself," I said.

"You look it," laughed Carlos.

"And if I win, you can go on and kill Benny. He's a pest anyway."

"Must not love him enough to risk that," Carlos said.

"Hell no." Again came that pathetic whimper, and I could smell the hot tears which were now streaming down Benny's fluffed cheeks.

"Well, no fur off my nose," Carlos says. "How much you got?"

"Thousand," I answer, to which the reply was a hearty gust of laughter from everyone around. "It's the best I could do."

"I bet. Still small potatoes..."

I grin. "But enough for you to back down from a fight, huh

Carlos' eyes widened, and his whiskers twitched. To my left, I heard Benny gasp, reason coming back to his dim eyes. If he'd had his mouth free, he'd have screamed at me to get out of there, stop being stupid.

But I wasn't going no damn where.

I had Carlos right where I wanted him.

The rat chuckled. "Elric, a chair!"

I sat down and tossed in two hundred, then lifted the cards into my paws and peeked at their undersides. I had a King and Queen of Hearts, two Spades, and two Aces. Licking my lips, I quickly glanced at the others around me and Carlos. Their tells weren't obvious, but one had a vein pop out along his forehead between his ears, and another hesitated and considered, scratching the bottom of his lower flew. The other guy scratched his cheek and threw down three hundred dollars, with Carlos raising it to four hundred.

Too much for me, so I folded. Benny saw this and screamed behind the ballgag in his mouth, but I flashed him one of my trademark grins to calm him down. The other two at the table followed after a couple seconds, the cards dropping to the table like raindrops on concrete. Carlos laid down his cards and laughed. A two-pair of 10s and Jacks, a respectable hand that freaked all of us out. I cussed myself in my head, I had to get my ass in the game as I felt my ears get hot from frustration and embarrassment, as I was well aware that I was about to lose already. I stayed for the next game, throwing in forty this time while everyone was high stakes.

I thought I was good, placing three cards on the table: 2 of Diamonds and a 10 of Hearts. I got cocky; this wasn't bad at all and raised my pot by ten. The next was an Ace, and I asked for another. A 4 of Spades. I felt good, but lost my nerve when

Carlos raised the bet by a hundred and so I folded. Carlos laughed as I watched him lay his cards out in a neat row, a 3 of Diamonds and a 3 of Clubs.

I could've beat him.

Carlos laughed. Benny grunted in shock and lowered his head, ears folding flat against his skull as he realized that that hope he'd had was getting pretty damn dim.

"Shit," I said.

"What's it gonna be, Tommy DeCarlo?" Carlos said. "You got a chance to walk out of here while you still can, on your own two feet and on your own power if you just call it right now. I'll keep Benny here for a while longer until I have Elric gouge out his eyes and make love to the empty sockets."

Again came that pitiful scream from Benny.

I growled.

That wasn't gonna end this way, at least if I could help it. Like I said, I owed Benny and wasn't about to let his fate be some asshole's fuck toy.

"Can I cut the deck?" I asked. Carlos raised an eyebrow as he looked down at me. "It's throwing me off that I haven't shuffled. Usually I get some mojo from it. You know, superstitions."

The others looked to Carlos, who looked at me then at my paws. "Can you even do it?"

I flashed a toothy smile and snatched the deck with my left paw, shuffling and cutting all in one go. "I think I can handle it," I replied and laid the deck back down on the table's surface. What I hoped he wasn't checking was a trick I'd picked up, called an "anchor shuffle." Kind of like dealing from the bottom of the deck, but instead I shifted my Aces into a slit I'd cut into my cast. To Carlos and the other guys' eyes, they'd see nothing was up.

That was the hope, at least.

Carlos wasn't smiling as he took his cards and looked at them. The rat set his jaw forward and wrinkled his small whiskers. "I'll bet four hundred," he said, sliding his money to the center. One by one, the other players folded and rose from their chairs. I was looking at my deck, a frown folding deep along my muzzle as I glanced back at Benny, who was watching the whole thing play out and trembling against his milking.

"I'll raise you...five hundred more," I said.

"I'll raise you three hundred more," Carlos shot back behind a grin. "I'm sure you had to do some things to get this money, huh?"

"Maybe so. It was a neat day for me, but if you hear something nine months from now about the waitress across the street talking about some mutt who got her knocked up, you never saw me ," I answered.

Carlos smirked. "I'll remember that." Returning to his cards, he added, "You should've left Savio alive. You could've made a cute couple."

"I sincerely doubt that," was my answer, taking the moment as Carlos was looking down at his cards to shift one of mine from the cast and up into my paws. "Savio was a dick."

"Hah, sure was," Carlos said. "Always keep your friends close and your enemies closer. Got to say, it's honorable you're here now to save your frail."

"I owe Benny," I answered, and slid the whole pot to the center. "I'll raise the whole thing."

"And I'll meet that," smiled Carlos, holding his cards in the air. An Ace, King, Queen, Jack, and Ten of hearts "Straight flush, hotshot."

"Shit," I grunted, looking down at my paws. I sighed and threw down my cards. I heard the creak of chairs as everyone looked at what I had laid across the surface.

Five Aces.

Royal flush.

I raised my head and grinned wide.

"I beat you, old man," I said.

Which brings our story back to the present.

Carlos had gotten up from the table and was over to Benny, stroking down his back. The dalmatian was wincing beneath those touches; I couldn't blame him, but honestly I'd been just as rough too and figured at least Carlos had taken care of him this whole time.

"You did good," Carlos continued as he swirled his drink in his paws, taking a deep sip. "No one's ever beaten me like that."

I smiled. "Always a first time for everything."

"Truth. Everyone else gives up. But you had strength. Stamina. Staying power. Cunning, even."

"Just lucky I guess."

Carlos smirked. "Well, lucky you. Don't know how long I'd have kept your friend here anyway. Whining and complaining like he does."

"Yeah, he can be a pain in the A," I agreed walking towards Benny, who was laughing behind his gag. Carlos hadn't turned off the machine and I watched as another trembling orgasm shook through Benny's body and the pump took his milk and turned into "the Milk" for Carlos' clientele, Benny's dick head so swollen and red that it looked like a ripe cherry for the pickings.

"I like you Tommy," Carlos said while he mixed the drinks for us. "As promised, he's all yours."

"I'm glad for that," I said, as I ran my good paw over Benny's torso. I saw the hope and relief swim in Benny's eyes, and the patient waiting for when either I or Carlos would turn the machine off and let him go.

"You know I didn't mean what I said, right?" I said into Benny's eyes. He tilted his head in that cute fashion that I'd come to know so well over our long relationship. He knew what I meant. I grinned. "The truth is you're *really* annoying, and I owe you for getting me into this whole mess."

Benny's eyes reacted where his body couldn't when I reached behind my ruff and pulled the scalpel out. I sank both blade and paw deep into Benny's stomach and curved upward in a savage cut. Benny groaned and screamed behind the gag and I shushed him, holding the back of his head as his blood and intestine spilled out and all over my feet before his eyes–wide at one end, dilated at another–began to turn up white and roll up into the back of his head.

The milking machine had not stopped and was now turning a dark red as blood filled the tube. I then cut the ballgag off of his muzzle and his breathing comes at me hard and fast.

"T-Tommy...why..." was all he could ask.

"Because," I answered, "I never loved you, and you were always too much of a nag for me." With a speed that came with measured practice from playing cards, I severed his dick and ripped it out from the pump. Benny screamed wide as I jammed his cock down his throat as deep as I could, listening to him choke on his own blood and cock and thrashing and thrusting it in and out until I felt the dalmatian go limp as a noodle.

Carlos was standing behind me, holding the twin glasses.

He was laughing, big and deep.

"I do like you, Tommy DeCarlo!" he said, then shoved the glass into my good paw.

Studying the old man's eyes, I waited for him to be crazy with rage.

If I was a bold fucker I'd turn it down and take my winnings and get out of there. But that was if Elric wasn't waiting for me on the other side to beat my ass for beating his boss.

And plus I knew it'd be rude to just turn him down like nothing had happened. He did let me play him again and do all this shit just to have a chance at assuaging my ego. I admit, I kind of felt bad about Benny, but I figured that Benny would understand.

I won, and the odds were back in my favor again.

I'm a smartass, not a dumbass, so I knew what the odds were and I drank it down, and the minute I did I felt something was very wrong.

The smell was off, tasting like bitter almonds, and the room began to spin almost on instant. Sound was disappearing, like someone had turned down the volume and stuffed cotton up inside my ears while the room was growing dimmer and dimmer.

I was about to black out and just before my legs turned into jelly underneath me, I felt strong hooves wrap themselves around my body.

"The boss likes ya a lot, Tommy," Elric said, his voice echoing faintly inside my head, the silhouette of his horns fading with each second. "But I don't think you get why I didn't just kill ya the second you rolled back in here."

Carlos frowned. "The anchor shuffle, really, Tommy?" He tapped my cast with one long claw.

I can't tell you what was in the drink. All I know for sure is that it worked like a son of a whore, laying me out good on the floor of Carlos' room. When I came round, I had all my senses—smell, sight, taste, hearing—intact, except one.

Touch.

Reason for that became obvious when I was able to lean

down and see my hindlegs missing below the thigh, stacked up like kindling off to the side, as I saw Elric raise the machete up over my head and then drop it down on my left forelimb like a hammer. Pretty sure I vomited, and I vomited again when I heard the loud hissing sound come and the burn from the torch scorch the edges of my eyes as it seared the amputation shut. Smoke rose the wound before Elric was satisfied and raised the big machete to make the right match the left and I passed out from the pain.

When I came to the next time I was in a bathtub, again stripped. Carlos was leaning over the rim and looked at me, then directing four different sets of paws to get to work. I tried to scream, but tasted blood; my tongue had been cut out. I tried to struggle, but there was no feeling in my forelimbs, hind legs, or even my tail. Everything was like a dead stump of wood, which worked well as Carlos' assistants cut and carved the fur off my body with water and pocket lasers. Had I the sensations, I'd have screamed my head off, but could only watch as the blood rolled down my naked flesh to fall down the drain.

Elric came back into my view this time, and I saw him reach over me, checking a tube. As he did this, I felt my air being constricted and it dawned on me then that the tube was running from my nose, with another shoved down my throat. The bull moved over to another side of the tub and was checking a box, pumping a piss-colored liquid which was connected to the tubes and slowly making me drowsy. Before sleep came over me once more, Elric said, "Nighty night," and had in his hooves a big bag of wet concrete which he began pouring over my body.

I eventually passed out one final time and when life—or the weird facsimile of it—came back to me, I became aware that I was still in darkness. I couldn't move, and then I remembered what had occurred earlier, glad that I couldn't see what all the mutilation had done to me. I had no idea what time it was or how much time had passed. Then I heard footsteps, which sounded like they'd paused in front of me on the other side of the darkness and was quickly followed by the sound of a power drill coming in through the dark. The bit stopped inches from my eyes, and it was then that I knew I was encased inside concrete, smelling the dusty sweet mustiness, like a mix of wet paint and heat coming off the surface. My eyes parted the dust once the drilling stopped; I could make out the silence of the Electric Sewer. No one was around, and seats were stacked on tables. I was not able to look far or wide, but then I saw where Benny and I would usually sit and it clicked in my brain what had happened and where I was at.

Then a figure came out in front of the newly drilled eye holes and looked at me and laughed.

It was Carlos. "Hope you can breathe okay in there. I've made sure to get your oxygen supply at the bare minimum. Same with food and water." I felt him jiggle the tubes attached to my snout.

I listened to him snap his digits together, then someone pressed a finger against the twitching pucker of my asshole on the other side. It was snug, and they weren't gentle about it. I know that touch: Elric. The next thing I felt was an all too familiar sensation, as something slim, sharp and metallic was jammed up there. I wanted to scream about the scissors like I had when Savio did it, feeling them twist and thrust and forcefully widening the hole followed by Elric opening the pivot to spread the blades open spread me open. I couldn't scream or do anything, just exhaled sharply through the tubes.

"Jeezum Crikes how the hell did Savio fuck this ass?" Elric says behind me, voice slightly muffled but amused. I felt him shuffle around my wide, bleeding hole for a moment and then felt his thick, uncut dick pop inside me with no amount of ease or kindness, let alone lubrication except for my blood. I moaned out, groaning the best I could as the bull on the other end fucked me deep and raw, taking long and raw thrusts in and out of my backside. I felt it go at least a foot inside me, and my body was powerless to try to push him out.

"The tighter, the better," Elric said as I heard the hard moan follow and felt the warm rush of his cum fill my ass, wondering if the blood from my ass was making a sort of weird mayochup look. It was then that I noticed the low thrum that was equally familiar; I couldn't crane my neck down to see it, but then being aware of it I could feel its rubber sucker work my cock and pull me back at an incredibly high vacuum strength. Then a shock paraded through my body, and I trembled hard, feeling my cock grow harder as the machine edged the frenulum and head of dick and built me to a growing orgasm, overriding every sense in my brain to hold all of this back as the orgasm came and came hard. Electrical stimulation, never a thing I was into, the electrodes were attached at the base of my throbbing dick and balls and felt like a crazy, rhythmic beat, like hundreds of needles jabbing me again and again. Carlos held up the remote control and moved a dial, increasing the power as an intense rush of feeling hit my cockhead straight, finding a sweet spot, and I began to feel a spasm come over me.

"Damn, I'm gonna tell the boss charge a premium on ya," Elric says, his dick back inside my asshole which now felt a little wider.

I see Carlos turn his back on me to reach behind the bar. Then he brings up a camera to his face and begins snapping pictures. "Remember this? These are pretty indestructible, and it had some film left. Good thing too: like to commemorate moments like this."

Time moved slow as I watched the bar filter in, and I listened to someone order some "Milk." Carlos told them it was a new batch tonight that's called the Jack, a premium blend. I began to cum again, and the machine worked its hell magic and wouldn't let me go limp, while the e-stim refused to let me relax. Even with my stumpy limbs I still jerked and squirmed, with Elric laughing behind me, saying that I'd get used to it eventually.

"They all do," he said against the concrete block.

When someone else ordered the Milk from Carlos, I watched the customer—a bright-eyed tiger, wearing a mock-ruff of a lion—sniffed it and then looked back at Carlos.

"So you call this the Jack, eh?" says the customer. "That makes me think of the bare minimum card for any player. You're telling me this stuff is premium when it's named after such a wild card?" I watched Carlos as the rat nodded his head and began to draw my jizz from the machine and serve another customer. The tiger took one long sip and then another, then licked away my jizz from their lips and whiskers, saying, "Damn this really is strong, I can feel it going through me! Nothing minimum about that!"

Even as the tiger said, I felt the milking machine increase its pace, as Carlos' paws dialed up the e-stim and milking machine each a couple more notches and Elric came again inside my ass followed by a new cock burying itself inside me. Something told me this wouldn't be the end. My screaming moans would never be enough to rise above the throbbing bass of Air Wolf's music or to penetrate the concrete that was my new home. I could only look out and see the line forming behind the departing tiger, tailing batting to and fro as he talked up the drink and caught the interest of those who wanted to try it.

"So what're you gonna do if you run out?" said another customer to Carlos, right as the e-stim shocked another orgasm out of me, and I came hard.

"Plenty more where that comes from," Carlos says, drawing the glass to a head and cutting the foam.

THE GLOW

LINNEA LITERALGRILL CAPPS

"You two girls made quite a sexy yin yang making out at the bar. Did you end up getting her number?"

Elyse sighed, ears turned down and outward at her roommate's question as the two left the Electric Sewer. She was used to being the center of attention wherever she went with her dusky charcoal fur. Melanism was incredibly rare in deer, so even with some of the bright colors others dyed their fur, most considered her an exotic curiosity that met her.

Tonight however had been different. All eyes had been on the curvy polar bear, including the deer's own. It wasn't the hypnotic sway of her hips as she danced nor her endless well of energy that drew such attention. Markings adorned her entire curvy body in intricate patterns that seemed to glow like the neon lights in the club itself. Neither Elyse nor the other patrons of the club had seen anything like it before.

The deer had always harbored a weakness for plush, soft ladies like the polar bear and had been determined to try her chances at flirting and dancing with her. Elyse had learned her name was Nicolette between bouts low grumbly giggling as the two danced together.

The only time Nicolette took a break from dancing the entire night was to go to the bar alongside Elyse to share a drink. Elyse hadn't managed a single sip of the club's signature Woo Woo cocktail before Nicolette had downed her entire glass. The polar bear had grasped her chin in one white and powerful paw and pulled the deer into a kiss. Their tongues had rolled over one another, Elyse tasting peach and cranberry tinged with alcohol. The deer had hooked her leg around the polar bear's waist, grinding into the polar bear as if to start the blaze of fire pooling in her lower abdomen. Nicolette had pulled back, their lips barely touching, growing dizzy as they breathed each other's air.

"Dance more with me?" Nicolette had asked, confusing Elyse to no end. She had figured at this point the two could return to her nearby apartment and finish the fun they had started. At worst, maybe they could claim a bathroom stall at the club.

"W-Wouldn't you rather take this somewhere private?"

Nicolette had pulled away, turning her eyes towards the dance floor and its myriad of neon lights. "The glow... it calls to me...."

Elyse had been flabbergasted as the polar bear walked away, returning to her wild gyrations to the pounding beats of the music. She had felt certain that Nicolette had to have been on party drugs of some kind.

"No... I didn't get her number Mica."

Her fossa roommate chirped in frustration. "Elyse, you're never going to get a girlfriend if you turn down signals *that* obvious!"

The deer crossed her arms, a single hoof stomping hard on the pavement. "She wanted to dance instead of actually continuing that makeout session. It doesn't matter if she was into me—I have to actually sleep so I can work in the morning."

Mica raised her paws in the air, a sign of surrender. "Alright, I can tell you're feeling a little beaver jammed right now, but don't take it out on me!"

"Oh my God, Mica, please never use the words 'beaver jammed' ever again for the rest of our lives."

The two laughed together as they continued their walk home, the apartment they shared close enough to the Electric Sewer that taking a taxi would have been wasted money.

"Still, how do you think she got her fur to glow like that? I've seen chemical fur branding before but nothing like that."

Elyse shrugged, having no idea either. She knew that to get fur to permanently change colors, complicated chemical brands had to be used. Body modders not only charged a premium price for the service, but it was supposed to be quite painful. Nicolette's body seemed to be covered with them; even her face had small markings. The deer realized the polar bear must have had a pain tolerance beyond what she could ever imagine.

The two approached their apartment complex, unlocking the door to get inside and taking the elevator to the third floor so they could get to their apartment proper. Elyse immediately went to her bedroom and flopped onto the bed with a sigh. Once she was certain Mica was settled in her own room, she reached under her bed and pulled out a vibrator wand she kept hidden there. If Nicolette wouldn't finish what she started, the deer figured she'd have to take matters into her own hooves. After she relieved that built up sexual tension, she could maybe get some proper sleep.

Her hooves were tingling, almost as if the flow of blood to them had been restricted and they were finally waking up. She felt more aware of those limbs than she had ever been before in her life. Had she slept on them funny overnight?

As she tried to roll out of bed and stand, a shot of electricity rocketed up her legs the moment her hooves touched the floor. The surprising jolt of pain made her fling herself back onto the bed, breathing heavily, afraid to look down and see if she had somehow broken something. The tingling was becoming more powerful, seeming to move her hooves all on its own, rotating them with her ankle.

It started as gentle circles but was slowly escalating, the tingling sensations somehow forcing her ankles into movement. Elyse tried to sit back up on the bed but felt her body being held down by an invisible force. Her ankles began to twist to their furthest healthy points, stretching and straining as the deer could do nothing to stop them. With a wet crunch the bones snapped, twisting her ankle into impossible right angles.

She woke suddenly to the sound of her alarm clock buzzing, wheezing with her tail curled almost painfully under her rump in fear. She panted desperately, trying to not work herself into a panic.

"Just a bad dream, just a bad, fucked-up dream." she repeated to herself, trying to get her heart to stop beating at too rapid a pace. She hadn't had a nightmare like that since she had been a young fawn. Still, she knew she must prepare for her shift at the No Doze Cafe making coffee as she did every morning. In the end the strange dream needed to be pushed aside, even if she swore she could still feel the tingling in her hooves. She had to make money to pay for her previous night out at the club, so she'd need to open up the shop for her early morning shift.

She got dressed and tried to quietly sneak out of the house to allow Mica a little bit more time to sleep. The fossa usually shared a shift with her at the cafe but only had to come in after the morning preparations were complete. Anything to save the owners from having to dip into their profits to pay a tiny bit more on Mica's paycheck.

Elyse wasn't a fan of having to do so much work on her own each morning, but the owners did let her have a free pasty and cup of coffee each morning she worked, and she couldn't deny the perk of a free breakfast. She got out of her apartment complex and began her short walk to work, hoping that getting her hooves on pavement would remind her brain that the prickling sensation in them had only been in the dream. As she approached the cafe, her eyes were drawn to the neon sign currently reading "Closed" that hung behind the window.

How had she never noticed just how beautiful it was before? Gentle glowing, red and vibrant, twisting through the glass letters holding in neon gas. Even with the sign telling all that walked by that the building was unable to be entered for business, she had never felt so warm and invited. Why was red considered a color to make people stop in the first place?

"Elyse? Elyse you need to snap out of it!"

Mica was poking at the deer with an extended claw, hoping the sharp point would wake her from her reverie without having to actually pierce her skin.

"Hmm?" Elyse shook her head rapidly side to side, trying to shake away the fog that seemed to be clouding her mind.

"How tired are you to be running this late? We don't have time to sit around, get the door unlocked so we can at least try and get some coffee going before we're slammed with customers!"

Had she really been standing there so long? Still, she knew Mica was right, and mumbled apologies while fumbling with keys to get the door unlocked.

Elyse and Mica had barely been able to keep up with orders, having to apologize profusely over and over for the long wait times as coffee needed to be brewed. It hadn't helped when a police officer had come in and had to hold up the entire line to ask about a regular customer that had gone missing, looking to see if they had come to the shop recently. The deer had felt so badly that she allowed Mica to take all of the scant tips they had received that morning for herself.

"It serves you right too, this is going to get me good and hammered at the Electric Sewer tonight!"

Elyse was once more enamored of the light in the window, not wanting to change it from the green letters reading "Open." They were so bright and green, soft, encouraging....

"As for you, weirdo," Mica mewed, interrupting Elyse's thoughts as the fossa clicked the switch on the sign with a paw, "you can go home and get more sleep. I swear if I come home and you're not in bed, I'm going to be pissed, got it?"

"O-Okay, Mica, I promise."

Mica's ears turned down and back, tail flicking as she gave Elyse a concerned look. "Are you sure you're alright? I could walk you home first."

The deer shook her head. "No, I feel bad enough I made work so tough today. You go have fun, and I'll get myself home and in bed."

"Alright, you get home and rest!" the fossa said, waving as she scampered away in her excitement to get to the club.

Elyse sighed, trying to fight against the pull of the sign in the window as she locked the cafe door and began her walk towards home. She hoped it was just from being on her hooves all day, but they seemed to be stinging even more powerfully than they had in the morning.

Elyse had been so distracted by the sensation she hadn't realized she had gone completely past her apartment and instead had walked herself back to the Electric Sewer. She gazed up at the blue and red lights showing the name of the club, slowly feeling drawn....

"No no no, you're going home and going to bed," she murmured to herself, turning around and stomping her way back towards the apartment, tail curling towards her rump. She knew she needed sleep, silently cursing Nicolette for the cold she must have caught from their makeout session. She kept her eyes to the pavement, trying to be sure she couldn't accidentally be distracted by another light as she made her way back to her apartment, choosing to skip dinner so she could just flop onto her bed.

She could feel the call to go and gaze once more at the neon lights. It was as though a voice in the deepest recesses of her mind was urging her to stand and go, to not stop walking until she found glowing brightness to bask in. It was as though the tingling in her legs were trying to move them for her, but she refused the sensation's nudges, not wanting to leave the warm comfort of her bed. Especially not when she felt like this.

Waves of warm static were pulsing from her hooves up the back of her leg, only ending once they reached her pelvis. It was as though an electrical storm was forming in her groin, building towards the lightning strike of pleasure that needed to be released. Elyse could ignore that the tingling was growing stronger, looking as though it would overtake her entire leg. Right now she had another part of her body needing her focus.

She shoved a hoof between her legs, hips jolting up in pleasure at the touch. She allowed her knees to curl, thrusting herself up with each movement of her deft hoof rubbing across her clit. She was becoming frantic, hearing just how wet and slick her folds had become, the spark of pleasure spiraling out from her groin from the skilled self-massage. The storm inside her was crackling to a fever pitch, static overwhelming all of her form, the lightning bolt about to strike!

With a blood curdling snap, her knees gave way, the tingling in her legs twisting them in a fast and powerful motion. It had been displeased that she had not listened to the glow's call, though whatever it was she could not figure out. She was too focused on crying out in terror and pain as her knees began to bend in the wrong direction, her hooves falling lifelessly to land on the front of her thighs.

Elyse gasped, rolling in clumsy terror from the bed and becoming snared in a tangle of sheets. She desperately reached forward to assess the damage to her legs, only to find once again she had been dreaming. The buzzing still continued however, this time more powerful than before. She groggily turned to look at her clock, seeing she was awake a few hours before she needed to be before her shift.

Still, the idea of trying to go to sleep again was far too terrifying to entertain. She decided to take a shower instead, hoping the warm water could soothe the gnawing sensations in her legs that refused to calm otherwise.

The deer untangled herself from her sheets, tossing them in a crumpled heap on her bed. She then removed the clothes she had slept in, letting them join the pile on her floor. She walked quietly to the bathroom, not worried that her sleeping roommate might see her naked in the dark. She was wondering when Mica had installed the night lights in the hallway to the bathroom, the pink glow lighting her way coming as a nice surprise.

As she walked into the bathroom, her eyes went wide as she saw the mirror. The glow hadn't been from anything plugged into outlets, it was coming off her own body! She looked down, her pussy still a bit wet from the pleasurable part of her dream. The tender parts of her flesh and clit were glowing pink, as were her nipples. When her mouth opened in surprise she could even see her tongue seemed to have the same electric pink quality.

She rubbed her eyes to try and be sure she was really awake. Once she reopened them, the glow seemed to be gone. She decided the shower could wait; if she was so sleep deprived or sick she was seeing things, it might be a good idea to call into work. She went to the kitchen, grabbing her phone to call up another opener at the No Doze Cafe to take her shift.

Elyse's entire body was trembling as she curled in on herself, rocking back and forth on her bed. Her entire body was teeming with the prickling sensations, the lack of sleep leaving her in a daze. None of the pain meds in the bathroom cabinet seemed to cut into the sensations, and the dreams had only gotten worse over the past three days.

Mica had been sure to keep the deer quarantined to the apartment, going out to get food, groceries, or whatever other things Elyse could need.

"This is one hell of a flu you've got. Are you sure you're not too tired to take care of yourself? I know my friend is only in town for one night, but I don't want to leave you alone if you're feeling this bad."

Elyse knew that Mica had been looking forward to this night on the town with her childhood friend for some time now. Despite having gotten no proper sleep, the sensations and fear of further nightmares kept her awake. The deer didn't want to be selfish and keep Mica from having fun, especially after how much the fossa had been doing for her.

"I'm positive, I'll be okay, I promise. Now go have fun. I'll try hard to get some sleep."

The fossa gently patted Elyse on the head. "Okay, if you're absolutely sure. I'll get the lights for you on my way out." Mica slowly walked out of the room, flicking the lights off.

Whenever the room was dark, it seemed whatever was

growing beneath Elyse's fur crept under her skin that much stronger. It disliked the dark, it craved the light. If she hadn't been so tired, she'd have sworn she saw bumps in her fur, almost as though something real and visceral was trying to press out through her flesh. This did not help just how impossible she found it to sleep, the sensations causing friction in her mind from the discomfort and tension building.

"Gaaaahhhh!" She slammed her hooves onto the bed in exhaustion, hoping this desperate display of frustration could somehow relieve her symptoms. She would give anything to have some form of relief, anything for a proper night of sleep once more, anything to stop the tingling that haunted her every waking moment. She began to sob, unable to hold back tears as she trembled and quaked in her bed. Eventually her body and mind could take no more, and she finally succumbed to slumber.

She could feel it once more, that overwhelming sensation that could not be escaped. It was calling to her, louder than ever before, determined to find release. It promised that she would be happy once again, calm once more, if only Elyse could give it what it wanted. Elyse was desperate to comply but lacked a clue as to how she could. What did it even want? What could shut it up, even for just a moment?

Then she remembered the neon sign at the No Doze Cafe. How she had felt so good, so comforted, so warm. Mica had told her it seemed like she was in a hypnotic daze, but at this point she didn't care. If it wanted the lights, the moment of relaxation would be worth it.

She gave in, finally letting the sensations take control of her movements. It didn't care if she only had on some sweatpants and a sports bra, it wanted release and it wanted it now. Once it had dragged her out of the apartment complex, she found herself surprised when it turned her body to walk away from the cafe. She tried to fight it—didn't it know the relief was the other way? It struck back hard, threatening to break her limbs once more. Elyse was not willing to argue, letting it fully take control once more.

When she approached the Electric Sewer, it dawned on her. There was nowhere else nearby with as much neon light for her to bask in. She could stand outside and enjoy the glow.

"Excuse me, ma'am?"

A black bear placed his powerful paw on her shoulder, startling her back into focus. He wore a leather jacket and denim pants, letting all the fur of his chest show out to the world. It was obvious he had been planning on dancing at the club that night.

"Do you mind? I'm trying to—well, to...." Elyse realized any explanation she could offer would sound crazy, like she was tweaking on some sort of drugs.

There was a bit of drool on her muzzle; she had to have been leaning against the wall, staring slack jawed up at the neon sign proclaiming the club's name. She could vaguely remember trying to get inside, but the bouncer refused her entry for some reason she couldn't remember.

The sparks that seemed to rocket across her entire body had turned to a dull buzzing. Even if she wasn't asleep Elyse didn't have time for whatever this bear wanted. She had found her temporary relief.

"The lights are only going to help you for now. The symptoms are going to keep getting worse if you don't do something."

The deer's eyes went wide. "How did you...?"

The black bear interrupted her, using his superior strength to pull her away from the wall and begin leading her away from the club. "You must have met my partner, Nicolette. It wants out right? Don't worry, I can help you let it out."

"W-Wait, my lights! Who do you think you a—"

"Jonas, Jonas Salk. Now come on, you'll like my neon brands better than any light. You have to let the glow out."

Elyse was confused but stopped fighting, trying to remember where she had heard the last name Salk before. Hadn't she seen the name on the news? Some famous epidemiologist?

Lost in her thoughts, Jonas had led her towards a body mod shop a few blocks away. Jonas unlocked the door, a tiny bell rang as they walked inside. The black bear flicked on the lights, still pushing her back further into a private room in back.

"Nicolette! I'll need your help down here."

Elyse looked around the room, noticing there was a large table shaped slightly like a cross that seemed to have leather cuffs to hold people down by their wrists and ankles.

"W-What's going on h-here?"

Jonas rolled his eyes. "I told you, we're going to let the glow out of your body. You want the buzzing to stop right?"

Elyse nodded, the sensations having ramped up in intensity since she left the glow on the club's sign.

"Good, then you'll strip and get on the table."

"Excuse me?" The deer was about to give Jonas a piece of her mind but then saw Nicolette walking into the room, the patterns in her fur glowing bright blue. Elyse was startled that she wasn't wearing any clothes, though she couldn't complain about the view. Even in her current state, she wanted to bury her face into the soft white fur of Nicolette's voluptuous chest.

"Oh, it's you! I did hope we might meet again. Now listen to

Jonas—you'll need these clothes off."

Elyse noticed that the polar bear's nipples and tongue were glowing, and when she glanced down sure enough her pussy was glowing too. It had been just like what happened to the deer in the bathroom days before.

"You have it too? The...."

Nicolette gave a knowing giggle, reaching out to start slipping off Elyse's pants. "The glow darling, you must become one with it. Allow it to mingle with the glowing lights, feel the euphoria."

Elyse was unsure what all of this meant but was not about to complain that a gorgeous naked woman was helping her strip down. Still, the glow seemed to call to her, and the deer couldn't help but lean her muzzle forward, using her tongue to lap over one of Nicolette's nipples.

"So eager!" Nicolette purred, using a claw to simply slice off the bra the deer was wearing, not wanting to pause the attention she was getting.

Elyse was using her paws to make trails in the velvety fur of the polar bear's belly, enjoying the soft fat of her belly underneath. She latched onto Nicolette's breast, suckling away. It was one of the only neon lights in the room. She knew nothing more than she needed it almost more than life itself.

"Come on, you two, plenty of time for that later. Let's get her on the table alright?"

Nicolette guided the deer to the table, pinning her wrists up above her head until Jonas came to grab them and get them into the cuffs. The two then secured her ankles tight, Elyse trying to struggle against them to get to the only neon glow in the room.

"Please! Please, I need more!"

"Don't worry, I can make you have your own glow. You'd like that right?"

Elyse nodded rapidly. "Of course! Anything! You said you could make it better–is this how?"

Jonas let out a dark chuckle. "Yes, it is. I can make you glow just like Nicolette. You've got the glow inside you. This chemical brand can bring it out. It's just going to sting. A lot."

Elyse whimpered, her tail trying to curl down but being stuck beneath her, trapped between her body and the table. "Is it th-that bad?"

Jonas grinned, showing all of his teeth. "Don't worry, I certainly know a way to keep you distracted."

Elyse hadn't noticed the polar bear had made her way around the table and was moving her muzzle towards her pussy until the polar bear's warm breath was teasing against it. Soon enough the flicking of Nicolette's powerful tongue against Elyse's clit had the deer distracted enough to not notice the overpowering metallic scent floating through the air. She turned to see Jonas pouring a vial of what looked like red glowing blood into the clear container he was mixing chemicals in, preparing several brands of stars in differing sizes and a crescent moon for use.

Jonas saw that she was looking and dipped the crescent moon into the mixture that now held an ethereal white glow.

"Not everyone can handle their whole body being branded; they go into shock. Poor tiny red panda didn't stand a chance. Such a shame–she had such a pretty purple glow. At least she's still useful for something, or at least her blood is."

There was a fleeting moment of remembering a police officer at the No Doze Cafe asking about a missing red panda, but it was interrupted by the sensation of the brand being pressed against the side of her eye. Then there came the sting, followed by the burn of a crescent being burned into her fur. She cried out but found the pain was dulled by Nicolette burying her muzzle between her legs further, parting her sensitive folds with her tongue.

Her eye was now framed by a pink glowing moon, and Jonas grabbed one of the star brands and dipped it into the chemicals before pressing it against her muzzle. Another burn, another shout, and another soothing from a tongue delving in deep. She struggled against her restraints with every touch of the brand as he made her body a pink starry night, but there was no escape, she was locked down tight.

Endorphins were starting to rush through her body, the brands while painful starting to dissolve into agonizing pleasure. Even as she writhed with each new mark made permanently in her fur, she didn't truly want to escape any longer. She tried her hardest to grind her hips to get the most from Nicolette's muzzle, feeling like a rubber band was being stretched in her lower abdomen, straining before it finally was allowed to snap.

Jonas jabbed his brand and held it tight on Elyse's breast, the extra sensitive skin jolting her back towards normal consciousness. He quickly dipped the brand to leave more marks on her breasts, then to leave similar marks on the other, only her nipples escaping the agony of the brand. The black bear began to then work on her stomach and towards her navel, forcing her nethers to clench powerfully.

Then Nicolette began to pull away, and Elyse howled in frustration. Why would she leave her in such pain, edging her to the point or orgasmic bliss only to once again force her to wait?

Then she saw where Jonas was aiming the brand next. Her eyes darted down to the slick fur of her pussy, but before she could form words of protest, he pressed the tiny star hard against her soft mound. Tears fell from Elyse's eyes, her blurred vision seeing another brand ready to mark her once more. Nicolette was helping her partner to keep the brands coming; there would be no respite between the brands on her most delicate parts.

Despite the excruciating pain, she could feel her pussy tense uncontrollably at every touch. A darkness seemed to be forming at the corners of her vision, but the glowing lights from her own body and the pleasure they brought were still bleeding through.

Her body finally plunged into orgasm. She felt as though her vision was fading to black, time slowing as she rode out the waves of pleasure crashing through her body. When her sex addled mind returned to focus, she could feel the straps being undone around her ankles and wrists. The pain was starting to sink in deeper, and she winced at every movement.

"Is it d-done?" she wheezed, trying to catch her breath.

Jonas's eyes lit up with a sadistic sparkle. "Sorry, hon, but we still have to do the other side."

Elyse yelped, the two strong bears lifting her up and forcing her onto her belly. The newly made marks were irritated at changing position, the deer feeling a gnawing itch from all of them.

"Besides," Jonas growled, moving his equipment so he could walk behind the deer, "I deserve a turn with your pussy too, don't I?"

Elyse could feel what must be the black bear's cock slapping against her ass, and she gulped in nervousness at just how large it was. Pain still emanated from her nethers from the rough branding it had suffered. Not to mention she had never managed to take a carnivore before, let alone one several times her size.

Nicolette moved to the front of the table, tilting up her muzzle until she could feel the heat of the polar bear's pussy radiating onto her nose. "Embrace the glow. Enjoy your transformation."

Elyse could feel herself drawn towards the bright blue glow once more, finding it nothing but natural to part the bear's lower lips and taste the juices of it on her tongue. The deer could feel the other bear aiming his cock against her own pussy, managing to force his tip into the velvety depths.

"Come on now, I want all the way inside."

Jonas took the brand and pressed it to the deer's shoulder blade, causing her entire body to writhe. "You want to be a good girl? Really feel the glow? Good girls get me off. Bad girls...."—he paused, placing a brand down on her other shoulder blade—"get more brands. You'll be a good girl, right?"

Elyse could tell just how much pleasure Jonas took in her agony and found deep in the recesses of her mind that she, or maybe it, liked it just as much. She tried to relax, remembering the kinky scenes she had played in before. She knew the more she got into the play, the easier the branding would be.

She took a trembling breath and relaxed, feeling her depths expand to take in more of the massive member throbbing inside her. There was another press of the brand, causing her to clench down around Jonas's length.

"Oh fuck, that's good, but Nicolette needs attention too. Good girls keep licking."

Elyse could hear the tease in his voice, knew he was preparing the brand once more, and worked to eagerly please the polar bear before her. She tried to gently lick and suck over her clit, loving how the polar bear's legs were beginning to tremble. Jonas kept jabbing her with the brand, thrusting in harder with each passing moment, determined to somehow put the entirety of his length inside her desperately clenching pussy.

The pain was melting into pleasure once more, Elyse feeling

eager to connect with the wet, glowing warmth before her, to please the unyielding hard length behind her. The static that had been tirelessly driving her mad over the past few days all was seeming to escape, leaving her body feeling elated after the days of torture. Her relaxation allowed Jonas to finally hit his mark, jolting her forward on the table.

She could feel him pulsing inside her, feel her pussy clenching to milk out every last drop of cum as he branded her fur with no mercy. Her face was lodged firmly between Nicolette's thighs, making it hard to breath. The world was no longer spinning on its axis, there was nothing but the purest delight she had ever known.

Nicolette and Jonas had rubbed a salve into her tender bits of fur as the three admired how she now looked like the darkest heavens with an uncountable number of pink moons. The polar bear went to fetch water, Jonas making sure that Elyse was actually going to survive the experience.

"The tingling is gone, right? Think you'll finally get some sleep?"

The deer was cuddling up against him, appreciating how small she felt against his large muscles. She had never known more exhaustion and pain in her life, yet she had never known a time she had felt better. "Y-Yes, especially after all of that. Th-Thank you."

"My pleasure. Just one more thing you should know: if you get under a lot of lights, it has a euphoric effect. Like the lights themselves are having sex."

Nicolette returned to the room, handing Elyse the water. "That's right, it's why I wanted to dance. To become one with the glow is marvelous."

Jonas couldn't contain a growling chuckle. "So I'm told, so go out, dance, and enjoy yourself, alright? If you notice anyone else really likes the light, tell them we'll happily help out."

"I still can't believe you got your fur branded like that!" Mica hadn't been able to stop mewing over the new hot pink accents in Elyse's fur since she had come home and seen them. The two had decided to hang out once more at the Electric Sewer, the deer secretly wanting to see just how fantastic the neon lights felt against her new brands. She had not been disappointed.

"Come on, don't you want to keep dancing?" Elyse was swaying in her chair at the bar, barely caring about the drink before her, wanting to lose herself once more in the glow.

"Really? Some of us can get tired you kno—"

Elyse couldn't help herself. She leaned forward to meet the fossa's muzzle with her own, forcing her tongue inside as if she were fucking her face with it. Her lust since entering the club had been insatiable, and she needed this small bit of release.

The fossa pulled back, the expression on her face making it obvious just how much heat must have been creeping up under her skin.

"I d-didn't know y-y-you liked me like that Elyse."

The deer giggled uncontrollably, grabbing her by the hand to drag her towards the bathroom and an open stall. Elyse didn't know it, but the glow was seeking to infect another host. Not that the deer would have minded had she known—its particular method of infecting was most satisfying.

NOT ENOUGH

THIGER

I met him in one of those ancient theaters; my memories of him are entwined with images of grain being projected on the screen, of old film badly restored, of white noise, of the fabricated memories of people long dead being replayed for our eyes, creating new memories in the present. The technology could recede, but the paintings, the poetry, the light, the music...those memories neither blurred nor faded.

He sat next to me on a day where every other seat was empty; it was the last time that picture would be shown, so everyone who wanted to see it had done so already. He had too, he said, breaking the silence. I gripped my seat tightly. First because the stranger had chosen to sit next to me. Secondly, because his smell overwhelmed me—that smell—a wolf. Male. My heart pounded harder. Still, he pressed on. He had seen me there before. I loved old movies, didn't I? I loved them enough to go to every single screening of this one, even though I must know it by memory. Slowly, painfully, I turned around to look at him, unable to resist that deep, crunchy voice, like cracking fire.

The wolf's black fur was illuminated by the shifting screen, making him morph, escape any delineation; he was like a distant memory, like the movies, whose characters played and acted over his face.

I saw the stranger regularly in the theater after that, and every time I could feel him inching closer, like a hunter about to jump, and even though I resisted, I inched closer, too. I knew that he knew, and it was only a matter of time. What I didn't expect was he would make his move on a crowded day. The theater was full, yet his arm crossed the threshold of our seats into that forbidden territory of the other. Wayward digits wandered down my arm until making contact with the paw at the end, my nervousness giving way to bold force as he laced fingers between fingers. I noticed he was missing a digit, with only a bandaged stump remaining, and my fur stood on end. There was stillness for one single second. Then he dragged my paw to his side, to his crotch, and made me touch it. Closing my eyes, and making an effort to keep my mouth shut as well, trying not to pant from the immense heat I was feeling all over, I explored. I seized him up, rubbed it, massaged it, cared for it, in a word, maybe, loved it, until it was alive and hungry, and so was I, so I went under his clothes and coated my paw in his hot seed.

That day we talked outside of the theater for the first time; Tom told me his name, and I mine. I saw him with a new clarity, but it was raining, so his muzzle was obscured again, a maelstrom of the lights from the street signs and lamps. Could I have saved you, had I made more of an effort? If maybe I had just reached out further, seen you as you really were, could I have prevented things?

One way or another, it was him who reached out–downwards, as he was taller–and put an arm around my shoulders, asking me if I had any plans for the rest of the evening, casually inviting himself along my usual route back home. He always took control, freed me from myself, made me his. I was always his. We walked like this the whole way, his arm denoting ownership, my embrace removing any semblance of doubt there could be to any passerby; and yet he walked with complete pride under the rain.

Over the following days, we skipped the old theater and met in my place every time, and every time I devoted myself to his pleasure. Exploring his body, I learned more about a person than words had ever achieved before; I tried, and failed, to count all of his scars, all of his bruises. He was wounded, yet no matter where I touched there was no sensitivity, only numbness. I dedicated myself to pleasuring him, but I could see he wasn't thrilled like before; not like in the theater, where there was the risk of an audience. Soon the sex took a step back. We started renting movies to watch after he brought a TV and a player, and we got to know each other outside of the physical aspect; and I loved all that he discovered in me, and I loved all that he changed in me, and all that he loved.

We usually met at night, and always at my place, a tall, ruined old building among other tall buildings. I was very poor and the higher-up rooms were all I could afford; the ones nobody wanted, where electricity was out half the time. I was high enough that you couldn't see the street from up there; I felt in an island of mist, surrounded by black pyres, those being the other worn-out buildings—and we were only lit by the pink or greens reflected from below. When I heard the knocking and I opened the door to find the big silhouette of the wolf towering above me, a black shape behind coming and going light, I knew everything was alright.

But I wasn't pleasing him. I started wondering about his wounds, why we never visited his place, or what he did through the day. Even if he didn't want to tell me, I wanted to surprise him, go above and beyond to show him my want.

So one morning he slept over; after he left while he thought I was still asleep, like always, I decided to follow him. I followed him all the way to the outskirts of the city, hidden by the clouds of mist of the morning. More dust clouding my view, like the grain of film, like the rain in the night. A clouded vision, one that didn't clear until we reached a lighthouse of neon signaling the entrance to a club. I first saw it reflected in a puddle, and I saw Tom enter the place in the reflection, distorted away.

I waited ten minutes staring at the signpost reading Electric Sewer, watching the light fizzle and crackle, before I went in.

I had been walking for a couple of hours, so it was past noon, and the place wasn't crowded, but it was open, all right. It was daylight, but the surrounding buildings covered it in dark. A couple dozen people were drinking, probably still from the night, and I saw cages for dancers, but they were empty. No sign of Tom. The music was slow. I approached the bartender, a rat, and asked him for something light to look like I belonged. I hadn't closed the door behind me, but someone did, and without its light I felt trapped in a void, the walls, floor and ceiling looking like one indivisible shape of black, the animals seemingly seated and drinking in the air, floating. I went deeper into that dizzying visage, moving into the darkness, slowly approaching another source of music.

I realized I was going down some stairs; then I was in a hall; then, when the music felt the loudest, I bumped into a door.

Inside, within the roaring music, was a fully lit white room. There were no decorations, no tiles; just pure white occupied by white tables and white chairs. There were disconnected screens in each one, and they all led to a stage where Tom sat at a circular table. This one, the center of attention, had a red cloth. Tom was smoking absentmindedly, staring up, out of it. There were other people, janitors, cleaning the absolute mess that was the room. Cigarettes, broken bottles and big stains filled almost every inch of it.

I walked up to Tom, crushing the trash, not getting but a look from the cleaners. The wolf looked at me with anger. I yelled a few things at him, but neither of us could speak over the music. Finally, he pulled me closer and spoke to my ear.

"What are you doing here?"

"Is this where you work?" I yelled back.

"Just go. Go, please."

"Tom..."

"You don't want to see any of this shit."

I pulled him even closer, hugging him, yelling.

"I don't care! I want to be with every part of you!"

"I'm not a janitor here."

"I don't care."

"You want to see what I do?"

"Yes."

"Liar."

"Yeah?"

I kissed him, with tongue. He growled, but he pushed me back, spreading his legs. I could see I hadn't had an effect. His eyes were defying me. This was a test. I had to show him I was up for it. I had to show him I would be in his world—give him what he wanted, there, surrounded by people. What really thrilled him.

I dropped to my knees, nuzzling his crotch and making a show of sniffing loudly around it. All I could smell was the place—the sickening cigarette, the cleaning products. All of it was disgusting. I took out his cock and swallowed its flaccid length. When I looked up at him, I expected him to be unimpressed, bored, perhaps; I didn't expect sadness. He was shocked; I saw his eyes glisten. I had misread something about the situation. But no, I wasn't stupid; I knew he must be putting on some sort of show in that place, and it had to be sexual; and knowing him, he was probably serviced by countless people. I decided to make him happy the best way I knew how. I took a deep breath and then kept his cock in my mouth, circling it with my tongue, not removing it at all. Slowly, very slowly, he hardened. He grew and grew until I choked—I couldn't take his whole length—but I still kept it in my mouth, even though I gagged and my saliva came out. Finally, out of breath, I took it out, panting. It was leaking, full of life; it bounced on his belly, spraying my face with his precum. Soon enough I swallowed it again, grabbing his thighs and making myself choke every time, my legs shaking with pleasure, my cock making a mess in my pants.

It was not an easy environment. It was a rough floor. It was a rough job. An hour went by, and he was still hard, leaking in my tongue, and I was still swallowing. I didn't care. I didn't get up. I just kept on sucking, choosing him over my breath, over my comfort, over my life. Half an hour later, he came and I felt a hit of pleasure, swallowing several times with a shiver. When I looked up again, he was smiling.

"I love you," he said, and his voice was full of melancholy.

He took me out of the room. Once the music was shut off, he explained things some more. He worked at the club—it was a special room where high-paying people could go and satisfy each other when the strip show became too much.

"Is that it?"

"I sort of run things in this room," he said. That made me feel a little more relaxed, if he was just the boss.

"But what are you doing at a nightclub this early?" I asked.

"My, er... clientele is very particular. They like to come in here before the regulars do, free from prying eyes. People will start arriving in about an hour, so... you should go."

"I... see. This doesn't change anything, Tom. Really." I tried to smile.

"Right. Look, I know what you're thinking. I'm not a dancer, this place's not—it's not about sex."

"All I care about is if you are okay. You seemed very stressed out when I entered... I... want to make sure I don't see that look ever again."

"Really? And what are you going to do? Save me, or something? Fuck off, man."

"Maybe I'll just come here in an hour, be a part of your work."

"No. If you do that, we're over," he said, with complete seriousness.

"Do you think I'm not up for it?" I asked, stammering.

"Yes. You're not."

"Let me prove it, then. I'm not going to back away, no matter the 'particulars.'"

Tom thought it over for a minute.

"Alright. If you want to prove it... let's do this, again. Come over every morning, help me relax before work."

"Yes, Tom," I said, my eyes fixed on his, my cock throbbing. I had felt a rush I didn't know when he came—like all of my struggle had been worth it for him. His cum had never tasted better. I knew that if it could keep tasting that way, I would be there for him, no matter how much he asked for.

"After work, I will still be going home," he said, and I quivered from the way he referred to my place as if it was ours. "And I'll still want sex. It won't be sexy. Your mouth will get sore. The second time it'll take me longer to cum."

"I don't care," I said. "I don't care, Tom."

He didn't say anything. He just turned to the door and opened it, and, before leaving to the other side, said one more thing. "Just remember. I don't want you here while I'm working."

"Yes, Tom," I said.

When he came home that night he was exhausted. That look I had seen many times before, that vacant eye, was explained now. The least I could do was be there for him. He said he'd take longer to cum—but when I suggested skipping the shower and just dropping his pants for me, right there against the door, he ended faster than before. I could taste piss and sweat and other foul odors, but I made him grab my head with both paws and thrust away, his speed slowly gaining confidence, slowly testing how far I would go, until he saw that I meant it, and he came in my mouth and I shivered just as strongly as before.

That became a new routine. Every morning I would go to the Electric Sewer and pleasure him, get him ready for the day; I suggested doing it before he left home, to spare me the trip, but that wouldn't do, no; what he really got out of it was the way he could introduce me to his world. Soon the blowjobs were moved from the white room to the main one, where regular folks were drinking; those weren't like the janitors, and a crowd would form around sometimes, and I'd have to battle my shame away. Eventually they recognized me as soon as I entered, which made me feel proud, in a way, because I was dedicated entirely to my boyfriend.

One time I wondered about Tom's payment, considering his clientele was 'exclusive.'

"It is handsome," he conceded.

"Then why are we here?" I said, pointing at my badly-lit, run-down home.

"I don't like money, man. I don't like owning it—I don't like using it. It makes me closer to them...the rich fucks that visit the white room. I don't want that association. I don't want to feel like one of them. I feel peace here, at home, in the dark." Then he added, "With you."

I didn't pry any further. He didn't pry into my business,

either—the fact that I never worked. The truth was my parents were willing to send me the smallest amount of money as long as I stayed away from them. I didn't need any more; for the longest time I was content watching films, one after another, mindlessly. That is, until Tom came around.

He would be laid back in the morning, but when he came home at night he was the opposite: angry, restless, and rougher. We started trying things out; tying me up, making me wear a plug, a mouth opener, a cage. It even leaked to the mornings, when he suggested we walked to the club together, carrying me with a leash. Things got rougher and riskier, until one day he was kissing my neck and it turned into a bite, and he dug deeply enough for blood to appear. I squirmed, moaned, but didn't stop him. I had been wondering if he'd make the leap to practicing pain. I had decided long ago I wouldn't refuse.

But he never asked for it outright, and yet, I wasn't being enough. His mood worsened; he came home angrier every time. What I did just wasn't enough to revert the damage that happened at the club. In the mornings, when we both sat at a drinking table at the club, he started ordering stronger stuff—patches that would give him crazy highs; the neon colors would be screaming, he'd tell me; if it was raining, he said it was deafening, even though there was music inside and the rain was nothing but a background murmur. Eventually, I tried out the patches too, wanting to feel what he felt, and it was like the film grain from my movies appeared over my eyes, and all the lights shone as if reflected by glass; I cried, that first time, and I went outside and I looked at that big neon sign reflected on the puddle and I stepped on it, deforming the image, wanting to do away with it all.

I wasn't enough. My love, my body—none of it was enough. If he wanted sex, that I could give him, but one day, even that stopped. One evening he came home with a bruised eye and a bleeding mouth, not wanting to do anything; I undressed him and saw new wounds all over his body—and then I saw the worst thing. He was missing another finger on his paw. The club had to stop.

"No," he said. "I can't quit."

"Why not?" I said, crying.

Tom smiled, rubbing one of his bruises.

"Because this is what I deserve."

Those words rang in my ears until I fell asleep. When we slept, I hugged him as tightly as I could, hoping perhaps I could keep him by my side, as if that was the last time I would; outside, a Saturday morning cartoon advertisement was heard despite my altitude, as it was projected onto the buildings.

When I awoke he was gone. It felt different. I knew what it meant. If I had already lost him, I had nothing to lose by visiting, then, by taking a look at the work done in the white room.

As I understood it, the daylight shift in the white room was beyond exclusive. I didn't have the money to afford my entrance, but Carlos, the rat owner, knew me by then, and he knew I was with Tom. I thought about pleading my case, but his lifeless eyes told me he wasn't an idiot; he knew about everything that was going on, and he didn't care. I was allowed passage into the room.

In action, the white room wasn't white at all. The lights flickered back between black and a series of rotating colors—red, cut; pink, cut; purple, cut; blue, cut; back to red. As I entered, a group of naked animals surrounded me, all of them wearing masks of species different from their own. They groped me from all sides; I fought them off, but they got some patches on me. I started to feel dizzy, and I fell on a table, watching towards the stage, unable to move. The film grain came back again, covering that flickering black, that series of photos in movement. I saw the sequence that was my boyfriend up in the stage, surrounded with cameras that replicated his figure on every screen on every table.

A dozen masked animals were all over him, most of them old, wrinkled and obese—the kind that could afford that place. It wasn't what I had pictured—he wasn't running the show; he was the show. He was tied up and patched up, looking absent as he was penetrated with cocks, toys, blunt objects, a whole fist. His cock was stimulated until it came, then came again, and yet the stimulation continued; he started groaning, crying in pain with as little strength as he could muster, but people continued using his body. I tried to move, but I could not. I understood why he had freaked out when I had gone down on him in that room; I had misunderstood his role. The only thing he had ever been able to dominate, to have control over, was me. The action went on, as I lay powerless. I was watching another grainy movie in that old film theater, unable to pause or rewind, and the images were reproduced on every screen, forming a kaleidoscope that prevented me from looking away. Someone started hitting him. Someone pushed his mouth too far, and he puked. They got more patches on him, and more. Some used needles. Eventually, they laid him on the table and took out knives. The crowd stepped back from their groping in expectant anticipation, giving the specialists their turn. My nose twitched from all the sex that floated around the room; every customer who wasn't on the stage was happily masturbating at their tables. All of them but the people handling the cameras, recording coldly, silently, professionally as the others started cutting Tom's parts. They started with one of his fingers, and then everyone stayed still, tingling as they heard the deafening screams. Then they went further, opening him up and exposing him to the cameras, showing him off, like my boyfriend was truly a beautiful thing. I remembered his words, "This is what I deserve." Tom stopped screaming. I closed my eyes and passed out amid tears.

I was woken up by Carlos. The room was white again, populated by the janitors at work. There was no music on, just a constant buzzing. Coming off of the patches, still seeing some grain, I was disoriented for a moment.

"Tom," was the first thing I said. My mind refused to remember; I didn't want to remember. "Is he okay?" And then, before he could reply, "He isn't just a sex worker, is he?"

"No, pal," said Carlos. "These clients–they were high society. This room wasn't about a strip show or just sex–it was about doing whatever they wanted to a body with no consequences, for the right price." He whistled. "And the movies we got out of it were a hefty extra."

In the center of the stage lay a black bag–over a puddle of blood.

"That's your trash, buddy," said Carlos. "I ain't gonna take care of it. It's your problem."

"Tom," I said, blinking. "Tom. Why did he do it? Were you...blackmailing him, or..."

"You wish. Truth is, he grew up here. We got him off the streets–He wanted to do it. He *asked for it* every time."

Tom's words kept ringing in my ears. *This is what I deserve.* He hated himself so much that no punishment was strong enough. There was something about the way he dominated me–his initial clumsiness, how he improved tentatively, trying out new things. I was the first person to have ceded before him, to let him take control of something. He was too good to fight back against his circumstances; too good for Carlos, those fat, old people, or the Electric Sewer. He was better than me. I could not manage the same restraint.

I jumped against Carlos, throwing him against the ground and aiming my fangs at his neck. I never made it there. The cleaners, inconspicuous as they had been, were over me in an instant, dragging me away. I yelled and shrieked at the rat, but the cleaners just placed patch upon patch on my fur, making everything fade away.

"You little bitch," said Carlos, as my senses dwindled. "We'll see how the crowd likes you."

I could not hear. I could not think. All I could do, lying on the filthy, cigarette-filled, cum-soaked floor, was stare at one of the screens as it played last night's video uncut. All I could do was watch Tom screaming all over again, but nothing about it felt real; he was just the memory of a dead person. The film grain captured the shots, the poetry, the lights and the music and would make them immortal every time someone decided to play it.

SHARP

THURSTON HOWL

Simon was hoping he wouldn't have too much trouble tonight. The bouncer nodded to him when he went in. The boar had a reputation here: as a member of the local gang, the Razors, Simon wasn't the type to be messed with. Two hundred pounds of muscle and fur, he had fucked up countless guys and girls over the years. Once, a guy had called him a faggot here at the Electric Sewer. Simon had held the horse's face down to the table, pulled out a razor, cut the horse's tongue out, then used the tongue as a bloody condom while he fucked the horse's ass. He tipped the bartender Carlos extra that night for cleanup. Another time, Simon had found out his brother had been cheated out of money by a drug dealer from the rival gang, the Pentagrams. The Satanist gangcult had been butting heads with the Razors for half a decade, and Simon wasn't too happy to have had his own family slighted by the group. When he learned one of the Sewer's strip-dancers was part of the Pentagrams, he paid her handsomely for a VIP private session. Telling her he was into some kinky shit, she obliged and let him tie her down to the bed. When she demanded protection before being fucked, he shoved his week-worn socks into her mouth and duct-taped over the Dalmatian's snout, rolling it around and around. He bred her hard and deep, wrote the word "cumdump" on her belly, and left the door open for others when he left. Word was that the Pentagrams were not happy their main moneymaker at the Sewer got knocked up with no idea who the father was from that night. But that was over two years ago. Water under the bridge.

Since then, the Pentagrams had steered clear of the Sewer, and Simon and the Razors reigned. But he had calmed down since then, too. He had not gotten into any real trouble since that incident. He came to the Sewer once a week to engage in vice. Mostly drink and sex. While his drinks never changed—the neon purple Sloppy Seconds cocktail—his sex preferences changed. He was what was called a submissive top. He liked to be the one tied up, the one controlled. But he didn't like anything going near his ass. He liked his cock used till he busted up inside someone's tail or belly.

So, he found himself a table near the newest strip dancers, two green bear twins, nursing an erection in one paw and a glass of Sloppy Seconds in his other. The synths blared all around him, the constant singular bass beat pounding through his ears, through his body, making the world around him vibrate with color. The alcohol brought his blood to his face, and he licked his lips at the sight of the swaying dancers. Pressing their asses to the poles, they brought their faces close together and kissed, the siblings' tongues lapping over one another. It had been a while since Simon had fucked a brother and sister couple.

"Hey, Simon," a voice yelled over the music.

The boar turned around and saw the alligator bouncer behind him. Since the bouncer was standing and Simon was sitting, the boar's face was mere inches from the bouncer's caged cock. "What is it, Randy?" Simon yelled.

The gator sat down beside Simon and leaned his snout forward toward the boar's ear. "Hey, got a message for you, from the Pentagrams."

Simon's eyes widened. "The fuck do they want? We haven't seen their hide here in a while."

Randy looked around to make sure no one was listening in

on their conversation, but even if they had tried, it would have been hard to hear over the pounding synths. "Apparently, they heard the CyberSk8ers tried to fuck with your guys a few months back." Simon remembered. He hadn't been part of the drama, but there had been a shootout at another Razor's pad. A lot of injuries, but only a Razor was killed. Apparently, it had just been namecalling that started it, but since then, the CyberSk8ers were the next mark for the Razors. "Anyway, the head of the Pentagrams isn't too fond of them either. He's got a special delivery for you in one of the VIP rooms."

"A...delivery?"

"Yeah," Randy smirked. "He apparently mutilated one of the Sk8ers and has him in full gimp outfit for your use and abuse. He wanted to offer it as a peace offering."

"It?"

Randy nodded. "Yeah, that's what the Pentagrams have been calling the gimp. They want to do business at the Sewer again and promise not to mess with you anymore if you don't mess with them. If you choose to accept, I was told to give you the key and room number."

Simon was silent for a moment, feeling the neon alcohol already buzzing in his ears. Ending a gang rivalry definitely sounded like a good idea. Plus, it totally made sense that the Pentagrams would have had it out with the CyberSk8ers.

Simon's curiosity—as well as his drunkenness and arousal—was piqued. Slowly, he nodded and said, "Sounds like a good deal."

Randy motioned his head toward the back rooms and pulled a glistening gold key from his pocket. "Right this way, then."

Simon didn't question anything at this point. He had made a decision, and he was committing to it. If anything, he was proud of himself. He'd knock out two birds—his need to breed and a gang rivalry—with one stone. He imagined how proud his own boss would be at how he took care of this. It was his mess in the first place really, and now it was his turn to fix it.

He only hoped the gimp could both keep up with him and that the gimp was receptive to orders. He had fucked plenty of leatherboys over the years, but most didn't like to take initiative, preferring to lie there and be used. He wondered, too, how mutilated this gimp was.

As they walked across the dance floor, Simon finished off his drink and slammed the glass down on someone's table. He felt the buzz in his ears and the warmth in his cheeks. It immediately went down to his groin, and his hard-on pulsed against his leather pants, almost in time with the music. When they passed into the next hallway, the neon pinks and greens vanished, no longer reflecting off his sharpened tusks. The narrow hallway was lit with a strong red light hanging in a corner of the ceiling. The light caught numbers emblazoned on each door. 1...2...3... The alligator led him to door number 6. Then, he handed Simon the key and walked away. Simon watched that reptilian tail swish in the red light as he walked away. Simon had no idea why Carlos made staff work bottomless if they were going to be kept in chastity the whole time. Defeated the whole purpose, Simon drunkenly thought as he unlocked the door.

When he pushed it open, his dick immediately went hard in his leather pants. This was apparently one of the kink rooms of the Sewer. On one wall was a St. Andrew's cross. On the opposite was an open cabinet with sex toys and BDSM tools on shelves. The sole light in the room was a singular red light bulb that swung from the ceiling, occasionally flickering and bathing the room in flashes of darkness. It reecked of blood, sweat, piss, and musk. He almost gagged from the smell alone, but, at the same time, it made his boner throb even harder. One corner of the room held three or four used condoms and a yellowed jockstrap.

In the center of the room, however, was a flat bed, probably just a huge wooden slab covered in leather and a thin layer of cotton, the underside of the bed functioning as a lockable cage or kennel for disobedient subs. Sitting on the bed was the gimp, facing the back wall. The figure was covered head to toe in leather, only its fingers, tail, horns, and exposed ass visible from this angle. The leather had intricate flower patterns over its surface, and the gimp's slender, curving figure made Simon think this had to be a girl, though the horns gave him some pause. He could not see any mutilation at all, and he wondered if maybe Randy might have exaggerated what the Pentagrams had said. By the gimp's horns, he could tell it must be a goat of some kind. He closed the door behind him.

As he made his way around the room to see the front of the gimp though, his heart leaped in a bit of fright. There was a hole in the front of the gimp's mask, allowing its face to be visible. While his peripheral vision also saw the goat's chastity cage was exposed–permanent, judging by the way the lock was melted shut–his eyes were glued to the goat's eyes. Where its eyes had once been, the sockets had, like the cage's lock, been melted shut, and large black pentagrams had been sewn into the malformed flesh there.

"What do you like, sir?" said the leather fleshlight.

Simon was speechless for a moment, but then he smirked. "Well, I'm told you're here to service me. Is that correct...CyberSk8er?"

The gimp nodded. "Yes, sir. I was told that if I didn't service you to your pleasure that I would be...," it hesitated and swallowed nervously, "...skinned and disemboweled...sir."

"Heh, sounds like something the Pentagrams would do." Simon's eyes could not leave the gimp's. "Well, how good are you at following orders, Toy?"

"I'll do whatever sir asks. No matter what."

"Good...good Toy," Simon said. "And what's to stop you from leaving or you doing something to attack me?"

The gimp smiled. "I was told you might ask that, sir. The bouncer, Randy, was paid off by the Pentagrams to make sure that if I left without you or that if you were with me but didn't answer a question only you and he would know the answer to correctly, then I would be held in custody until they could get a hold of me again."

Simon nodded. The Pentagrams were certainly sharp. "Alright, good. Well," he said, his head feeling fuzzier than ever as the drink worked its way through his system, "I'm in the mood for a good time. So, do exactly as I say, and I'll speak highly of you. You might get out alive, I dare say."

"Thank you, sir," said the goat gimp with a smile. "What would you like?"

"For starters, get off the bed, go to your right." The gimp obeyed, standing beside the bed after feeling its way over there. Simon got onto the bed and laid his head back against the meager pillow. "Now, here's how I want tonight to play out. I want you to restrain me to the bed. Then, I want you to pleasure my body. Pleasure my cock. Keep me poppered up. Then I want you to ride me till we both cum."

"Sir likes...to feel dominated?" the gimp asked for clarification.

Simon grunted. "Yes, now get to it. Restraints are on the shelf beside you." He started pulling his pants off, then threw his tank top to the floor beside the bed.

The goat reached over to the cabinet and pulled out four metallic cuffs. Over the next fifteen minutes, the gimp worked on restraining Simon's ankles and wrists to the bed. Every five minutes, the gimp would hold a bottle of poppers up to the boar's nose, holding one nostril closed to allow the man to get high off those for a minute. Even when the buzz started to mellow out, Simon rode out that high, only feeling hotter as he was stretched spreadeagle for the gimp.

It started by brushing its delicate paws along Simon's bare chest. It rubbed his tusks like they were dicks, made Simon suck on his short-furred fingers, then trailed them, still slick, down Simon's throat and over his chest. The gimp rubbed around the boar's nipples and occasionally pinched them. Still high, Simon whined, and the gimp pinched harder. Then, the gimp rubbed its paws around Simon's arms, feeling the bulging muscles there, before moving the paws down to stroke the boar's stomach, not as well-defined as his arms but still firm.

Without further warning, the gimp was massaging Simon's balls. The boar let out a deep gasp, and the gimp pulled softly on them, rolling them around in his paw. "Good, sir, you better breed me hard with these."

Growling, the boar said, "Damn right I will. Let me breed that ass. Please!"

The gimp smiled. "Not yet, sir. Not yet." The gimp was clearly enjoying itself as it stroked the boar's thick cock. The sensations left after a few seconds as the gimp made its way back to the cabinet, returning with two cock rings. One, it attached to the boar's balls, keeping them big and swollen. The other was rolled down Simon's cock, keeping him hard, his veins standing out. The gimp stroked him for a good ten minutes, never stroking fast, just enough to keep him hard.

Next, Simon felt the gimp put its wet lips to his cock tip.

Simon arched his back against the firm bed and struggled against the restraints. The goat was just focusing on the tip, sucking him on his most sensitive spot, unrelenting with how hard it sucked. One paw kept the boar's hips from bucking into the gimp's throat. Simon just had to tolerate the torture.

"Fffuck, please ride my dick. I need it!" he grunted and growled.

But the gimp ignored him, still just sucking his tip. It was equal parts tickling and edging. Yet, even as the boar squirmed beneath it, the gimp kept sucking on the tip of the boar's cock.

After another ten minutes of this, the gimp rapidly stroked the boar's dick, its paw going from tip to balls with each thrust, its saliva coating the veiny length. The boar squirmed and gasped against his restraints. "Nnnf, I'm getting close. Get up here, please!"

At that, the gimp stopped stroking altogether. Simon realized the gimp was teasing him now. But the gimp only came up to Simon's face, poppering him up again. When his cock started going back down, the gimp resumed its fast stroking. It took less than a minute for Simon to get fully hard again. He could feel cum swirling in his balls. He was ready to blow, but he had no intention of wasting that feeling on just a handjob, so he focused on keeping the orgasm at bay. He focused on the red light swinging overhead. He focused on the drumming synth that still echoed through this room. He focused on the warmth the poppers gave him, and, in that moment, he felt like he was out of his body. Yet, the orgasm still felt right there, right on the brink of exploding.

The gimp must have sensed this. The gimp stopped stroking and got onto the bed. It straddled his hips, its short tail hovering over Simon's knees. Its paw wandered over the bed and eventually to the nightstand beside the bed to grab a bottle of cheap lube.

Simon stayed quiet. He wanted to feel this. He wanted to be deep inside this goat now. This had been perfect so far, and he was ready for this moment.

The gimp poured a few dollops of lube onto its paw and then reached behind it to grab at Simon's cock. The grip was firm, and Simon tensed at the strong squeezing. His cock was already thick and red from the cock ring, but the touch still felt good.

As the gimp worked up and down his cock, the lube slathered all over him, making his cock cold, wet, and sticky. He moaned as his sensitive member was edged even further.

Simon did not understand all the foreplay and lubrication. Was this encounter the gimp's first time? Surely not. There was no way that someone who knew how to do this much teasing was inexperienced, but at the same time, it seemed more like the person was putting off actually getting fucked. Maybe the gimp was straight? Maybe they were like Simon, submissive but just not a bottom?

"Look, if you keep that up," Simon finally said, the poppers finally making his head start to hurt, "I'm gonna blow early. If you want that positive review so bad, I suggest you get on this dick. We can go multiple rounds, fine, but I need to cum *now*."

The gimp stopped stroking and wiped its sticky paw on the leather-covered bed, trying unsuccessfully to remove the substance. Then, the gimp got back in a straddling position.

"Finally," Simon said eagerly, wiggling his hips, preparing to penetrate the gimp at last.

Just when Simon felt his tip touch the gimp's asshole, the gimp opened its mouth. "But first, sir, I have another message for you."

Simon's eyes widened. "Wait, what?"

He stared into the dark pentagrams as the gimp smiled. "While it's true the CyberSk8es have had issues with the Pentagrams, we actually bonded over something...our dislike of the Razors."

"Oh, shit," Simon muttered under his breath.

"Unfortunately, I happened to be the...sacrificial lamb, I guess."

"Fuck you," Simon cursed. "Get the fuck off of me. *Now.* Or you'll really regret fucking with me." He pulled hard on the restraints, but they were locked in place good.

The gimp shook its head. "I'm afraid that's not in the cards. I didn't lie. If I tried to leave, I'd literally be skinned and disemboweled before they killed me. It'd be hell. And that's not worth it. This is much faster."

"What the fuck are you talking about? Get off me! Randy! Randyyyy!"

The gimp reached back around to stroke Simon's lubed cock a few more seconds while he spoke. "Here's the message for you, Simon. 'You always wanted to be a good Razor, but we're not convinced you've ever really had a good razor. Here's your chance. With love from a Dalmatian you once knew.'"

Even amid the boar's protests, the gimp slowly lowered himself onto Simon's hard length. Just with one inch of his dick inside the gimp, Simon knew what he was feeling. Rather than the usual fleshy insides he was used to when he fucked ass, he felt about ten loose razor blades inside the goat's ass. And, as the gimp lowered itself onto him, the blades pushed into his dick from different angles.

"FUUUUCK!" the boar screamed.

The gimp slowly bottomed out on the boar's dick and then lifted itself, then down again. Then up again.

Then down again.

Even as Simon screamed, blood poured out from both of them. Simon came in the middle of one scream. The gimp came just a moment later against its cage. But it continued.

Up.

Down.

Up.

Down.

Outside the door, the alligator counted out the hundred-dollar-bills he had been handed by the Dalmatian earlier that evening, just to deliver the one message, keep quiet, and not open the door marked number 6 till the morning. He heard screams coming from behind the door, but none of them were as loud as the hundred-dollar bills he fanned out in his paws. He sighed happily. Only bad thing was he knew he'd need to acquire *two* bodybags before the night was out. Walking back to his post under the pink and green lights, he was sharp enough to know that much.

POISONS

The following recipes were contributed by Red9. Each drink is based off one of the stories. Of course, make sure you are of legal drinking age before attempting any of these concoctions. Drinks at the Electric Sewer aren't for the faint of heart…or stomach.

HARE OF THE DOG

1 oz simple syrup
2 or 3 muddled cherries
2 oz whiskey of choice
Fill with ice
Top with coke

THE CONTAGION

1.5 oz of Tito's Vodka
2 oz cranberry juice
½ oz peach schnapps

SLOPPY SECONDS

1 oz simple syrup
2 dashes Angostura & Peychard's bitters
Muddle bright red cherry & orange slice
Fill with ice
2-3 oz favored whiskey (Buffalo Trace and/or Wild Turkey 101 recommended)
2 drops of purple food coloring (or a drop of red and drop of blue)

THE HEARTBREAKER

2 oz everclear
1 oz melon liqueur
1 oz pineapple juice
Fill with ice
Top with Sprite

THE SHORT CIRCUIT

2 oz favored red label scotch
2 drops blue food coloring
3 oz club soda
1 oz Sprite
Build in tall glass in order of ingredients.

NEON SUN

1 sleuce of absinthe or appropriate substitute
Turn glass to coat inner drum
½ oz simple syrup
2 dashes Angostura & Peychard's bitters
Fill glass with ice
2 oz rye whiskey
2 drops of orange food coloring (or drop of red and drop of yellow)
Garnish with lemon twist

MIX TAPE

The following jams were paw-picked from the writers of this book. Everyone contributed two each. And they've been the jams you've heard throughout the club all night. So give 'em a listen if you want. Here's a YouTube link for all you young'uns out there: https://tinyurl.com/electricsewer

"She Wants Me Dead" by Cazzette

"Desert Eagle" by Night Runner

"Lips Like Sugar" by Echo and the Bunnymen

"Dead Man's Autochop" by Specimen

"Just Can't Get Enough" by Depeche Mood

"Electric Groove" by Lazerhawk

"Dark All Day" by Gunship

"All Night" by Travis Something

"How to Make a Monster (Kitty's Purrrformance Mix" by Rob Zombie

"Wonderland" by Caravan Palace

"Dark Entries" by Bauhaus

"Fuck the Pain Away" by Peaches

VIP LOUNGE

Now, it's time to meet the lovely and sexy VIPs that told our stories tonight. Meet the writers!

CEDRIC G! BACON

I'm not much of a drinker, I'm the DD in any group and that always makes me stand out...course, there aren't many bats who will admit to not drinking anything stronger than a Bloody Mary, extra Type O plasma. I first came to the Electric Sewer when my friend said there was a pinball machine in the back...let me tell you, I found it, but I think it's weird that every time I shoot the ball I hear what sounds like someone screaming for help come from inside the machine. Must be hearing things, I suppose...

LINNEA "LITERALGRILL" CAPPS

I work the grill at the Electric Sewer. Didn't know we had a kitchen? Then you're not exclusive enough clientele. Still you might notice me walking through the club on my way back there, especially with all the metal in my face. Maybe if you're lucky I'll get Carlos to look the other way, let me take you to a back room, and mod up that body of yours. Have you ever wanted a split tongue? It hurts like a bitch but it's so fun after... Did you know that with a split tongue your taste buds automatically double in number? Sounds like...stop screaming... Sounds like something that could be true, doesn't it?

Oh, and never ask me where we get our ingredients. Trust me you don't want to know or risk becoming one yourself.

THURSTON HOWL

Most nights, you can find me working the pole. Hey, work is work, right? I give bondage discounts, and I give double discounts if you're a bull. Just sayin'. Anyway, gotta get back up there. The next song is my jam. Call me if you ever wanna be shown a good time.

NIKKOLAS JAMES

I bounce at the Electric Sewer even though it mostly bounces itself. I'm the last bendy thing you see before you black out. Biceps. Clipboard spectre at the door. Speak into the ear piece and enter through your exit hole.

RED-9

Working for Carlos is probably the best thing that ever happened to me. I was working as a bartender out in New Orleans, but since coming to the Sewer, I've gotten to really go all out with my drink ideas. Hope you enjoy. What? Wanna go to the back room? Well, let me slip Carlos something real fast, and I'll let you back here, yeah? Needing a break from that old rat, anyway.

THIGER

A roving outlaw that could never truly stay nailed down for long, I've rubbed shoulders with the lowest of the low and called them comrades–first cutting my teeth out West some decade ago and change, high time came to beat feet, and circumstance found me cozying up at the Sewer, atmosphere and attitude reminding me of some place from a long time ago... Maybe I'll be forced to run off again soon? Maybe not. For now, though, I

www.ingramcontent.com/pod-product-compliance
Lightning Source LLC
Chambersburg PA
CBHW040931050726
47507CB00022B/326
* 9 7 8 1 9 4 5 2 4 7 7 9 8 *